UP TO ME

The Bad Boys, Book 2

M. LEIGHTON

BERKLEY BOOKS, NEW YORK

THE BERKLEY PUBLISHING GROUP
Published by the Penguin Group
Penguin Group (USA) Inc.
375 Hudson Street, New York, New York 10014, USA

USA I Canada I UK I Ireland I Australia I New Zealand I India I South Africa I China

Penguin Books Ltd., Registered Offices: 80 Strand, London WC2R 0RL, England
For more information about the Penguin Group, visit penguin.com.

This book is an original publication of The Berkley Publishing Group.

Library of Congress Cataloging-in-Publication Data

Leighton, M.
Up to me / M. Leighton. — Berkley trade paperback edition.
pages cm. — (The Bad Boys ; Book 2)
ISBN 978-0-425-26985-5 (alk. paper)
I. Title.
PS3612.E3588U68   2013
813'.6—dc23   2013010604

PUBLISHING HISTORY
Berkley trade paperback edition / August 2013

PRINTED IN THE UNITED STATES OF AMERICA

Cover art by Knutson/Shutterstock
Cover design by Lesley Worrell
Interior text design by Tiffany Estreicher

To my husband,
who brings me happiness every day.

And to my God,
who brought me my husband.

ONE

Olivia

Out of the corner of my eye, I see the light flicker at the back of Dual. The door to Cash's office opens and closes as he comes out into the club. He looks up and our eyes lock instantly. His expression is carefully schooled, per my request, but that doesn't mean my toes don't curl inside my work shoes. His eyes are blazing as they look into mine. My stomach does a flip and then he looks away, which is a very good thing. Otherwise, it wouldn't be Cash who blew our cover, it would be me—when I leave my position behind the bar, march right over to him, plant my lips on his, and then drag him back to bed.

Tearing my eyes away from him, I force my mind back to my job.

Dammit.

"I got it," Taryn chirps, reaching in front of me to grab a dirty glass from the bar top.

I smile and nod my thanks, but inside I'm picking her crazy, dreadlocked motives apart. She's been nice to me all night and I'm not sure why. She's never been nice to me. Openly hostile, yes. Spitefully devious, yes. But nice? Oh no. Before tonight, I would've assured anyone who asked that Taryn would rather sharpen her toothbrush into a shiv and shank me than even look at me.

And yet, here she is, smiling my way and bussing my side of the bar.

Hmmm.

I'm not a naturally suspicious person, so . . .

Okay, so I am a naturally suspicious person, but I have good reason to be. A lifetime of schemers, liars, selfish buttmunchers, and all-around icky people has made me a bit jaded. But I'm coming around.

Anyway, I am extremely curious to know what Taryn's got up her sleeve. And there *is* something up her tattooed sleeve. I'd bet my life on it. Or her life. Either way.

I can almost see the wheels turning behind the blue of her almond-shaped, kohl-lined eyes.

The only thing I can do, however, is watch my back and keep my eyes open. She'll slip up and show her hand eventually. Then I'll know what's going on in that twisted mind of hers. Until then, I'm more than happy to let her kiss my fluffy butt and help as much as she wants.

"So," she begins casually as she makes her way back to me.

"Got plans for tonight after work? I thought maybe we could hit Noir and have a drink, get to know each other a little better."

All right, this is getting ridiculous.

I stare at her, working to keep my jaw from dropping open as I wait for the punch line.

Only there isn't one. She's *serious.*

"You're serious."

She smiles and nods. "Of course I'm serious. Why would I ask if I weren't?"

"Um, because you hate me," I blurt.

Dammit! There goes keeping my eyes peeled and letting her continue on with her ruse.

"I don't hate you. What on earth gave you that idea?"

Oh. My. God. Does she really think I'm that stupid?

I turn to Taryn and fold my arms over my chest. I'm not even supposed to be here. Cash and I just got back from my dad's house in Salt Springs, Georgia, a few hours ago. Gavin, the part-time bar manager of Dual (Cash's club in Atlanta), had my shift covered since Cash didn't know if I'd be coming back or not. And yet here I am, working to fill in for Marco when I should be naked, wrapped up in Cash's arms. I don't have the patience to play games.

"Look, I'm not sure who you're trying to fool, but if it's me, you might as well give it up. I'm on to you, Taryn."

She opens her pouty ruby lips like she's going to argue, but then she snaps them shut. Her innocently pleasant expression settles into something a little more normal for her and she sighs.

"Okay, I admit I was a little jealous of you when you started here. I don't know if you knew this or not, but Cash and I used to date. Until recently, we were still . . . resolving some things. I thought you might be trying to get in the way of that. But now I know you're not. Besides, I know he's not interested in you. He's got someone else on the hook, so it wouldn't matter, anyway."

That piques my curiosity. "Why do you say that?"

"What? That he's got someone else on the hook? Because I've seen him with a blond girl a couple times and he's been very, very distracted lately. And that's not like him. He's not the one-girl type of guy."

"He's not?"

"Oh, hell no! I knew that going in. Any girl who goes into a relationship with Cash thinking she'll change him or that she'll be the only one is dumber than a box of her long blond hair."

"Blond? Because of the girl you think he's seeing?"

Taryn shrugs. "Her, too, but Cash has a *type*," she says, quirking one pierced brow at me and holding up a pale twist of her hair. "Blond."

I nod and smile, trying my best to seem unaffected. Which I'm not, of course. Far from it. In fact, I'm so affected I feel like I might hurl right in Taryn's pretty face.

"What makes you think he'll never pick one of these . . . blondes and settle down?"

Her laugh is bitter. "Because I know Cash. That boy has wild blood. Guys like that don't change. And girls can't make 'em. It's just the way they are. It's part of why they're so irresistible, too. Don't we all want what we can't have?"

I smile again, but say nothing. After a few seconds, she grabs my towel and swipes at a wet glass ring on the bar. "Anyway, I'm over it. I just wanted you to know I'm burying the hatchet."

"I'm glad," I manage to squeak out past the lump in my throat.

I busy myself with early cleanup duties. Dual is less than an hour from last call. How in the world I'll make it that long is beyond me, but I know the first step is to keep busy. But no amount of busywork can silence the conflicting voices in my head.

You knew he was a bad boy. That's why you tried to stay away from him and not get involved.

I feel dismay curl in the pit of my stomach like a cold, heartless snake. But then the voice of reason—or is it the voice of denial?—speaks up.

After all that has happened over the last few weeks, how can you doubt the way he feels about you? Cash isn't the type to fake it. And what he's said, what you've shared, isn't fake. It's real. And it's deep. And Taryn is a psychotic bitch who has no clue what she's talking about. Maybe all that tattoo ink has gone to her brain.

While all of that is true, nothing I tell myself eradicates the feeling of unease that has settled into my bones. Into my heart.

One part of me—the rational, logical, uninvolved, hurt-too-many-times part—pops up to make matters worse.

How many times are you gonna fall for the same lines? The same kind of guy?

5

But Cash is different. I know it. Deep down. I remind myself that it's completely unfair to judge a book by its cover. No matter how much experience I have with similar covers. Cash's cover might be that of a bad boy, but the book, the *inside*, is so much more.

As I clean the grate under the beer tap, my eyes wander the thinning crowd and dark interior of the club, looking for Cash. Wouldn't you know that when I find him, a busty blond bombshell is throwing her arms around his neck and rubbing her skanky little body all over him. I grit my teeth against the urge to jump over the bar, march right over there, and snatch her bald-headed.

But my anger fades into acute distress when I see Cash smile down into her face. I see his lips move as he speaks to her and my heart springs a leak. It makes me feel somewhat better when he reaches up to unwind her arms from around his neck and then takes a step back from her, but it'll take more than that to get Taryn's unwelcome words out of my head.

Dammit.

My mood circles the drain for the next half hour. Even the fairly likable personality Taryn has adopted when she's not being an utter bitch doesn't help. I even start thinking to myself that maybe it would be a good idea to go back to my townhouse for the night.

A bit later, as I wash the sliced-lemons container on my end of the bar, I'm still pondering my options while debating the likelihood that I have undiagnosed bipolar disorder. A shot glass slides across the bar in front of me. I look up to see Taryn at my right, grinning, holding a glass of her own.

"Shhh," she says with a wink. "I won't tell if you won't. It's closing time, anyway." She pulls a ten-dollar bill out of her pocket and throws it down.

At least she's paying.

Normally, I would politely decline, but a shot to calm my nerves and ease my troubled thoughts sounds like a good idea. I wipe my hands on a towel and grab the tiny glass.

Taryn raises hers and smiles at me. "Salut!" she exclaims with a nod.

I nod and raise mine as well, and we both toss back our shot. I don't need to ask what she poured. The vodka burns all the way down.

Making a deep, growly *ah* sound, Taryn grins at me. "Come out with me. You look like you need a night of frivolous fun."

Before I can answer her, Cash's voice interrupts us. "Olivia," he calls from the doorway of his office. "Come see me before you go. There are a few things I need to discuss with you."

"Okay," I reply, my stomach tightening with a mixture of excitement, desire, and dread. He ducks back into his office and closes the door. I turn to Taryn. "Next time?"

"Sure," she responds pleasantly. "I'll just finish up and head out."

She wanders back down to her end of the bar, and it occurs to me that we might actually make it to being friends one day.

Go figure.

I piddle around a little, slowing down enough that Taryn can finish before I go back to "meet" with Cash.

"Ta-da!" she exclaims, throwing her towel in the sanitizer to soak. "All right, Livvi, I'm outta here. Wish you could come, but duty calls." She tips her head toward Cash's office and rolls her eyes. Grabbing her purse from the shelf under the counter, Taryn circles around to approach me from the other side of the long, black bar. Planting her hands on the shiny surface, she leans forward and gives me an air peck like she's kissing each cheek. "Night, doll."

I'm still struggling with disbelief as I watch her walk through the door and out into the night, dreadlocks swinging. I decide that dramatic personality shifts like that *can't* be healthy.

The instant the front door thumps shut, Cash's office door opens. He emerges, his expression hard and determined. With purpose, he crosses the empty room and locks the double doors behind Taryn.

For a few seconds, all that I've been worrying about for the last couple of hours fades away like the space his long stride eats up so effortlessly. I'm mesmerized just watching him, the way he moves. His long, muscular legs flex with each step. His perfect butt shifts behind the pockets of his jeans. His wide shoulders are square and straight above his trim waist.

And then he turns toward me.

I might never get used to how handsome he is. It might never fail to leave me breathless. His nearly black eyes bore hot holes into mine. They don't break contact as he crosses the room again, this time toward me.

He hops over the bar and lands beside me. Without a word, he bends, throws me over his shoulder, and carries me down the length of the bar and through the cutout on the other end.

My heart is pounding as he takes me through the office and into his apartment on the other side. My body is on fire with desire and anticipation for what's to come, but my mind is still harboring some doubt and insecurity from earlier. I'm debating whether to say something to him and go back home for the night or just ignore every shred of rational thought and stay, when he sets me on my feet.

Immediately, his lips cover mine and all other considerations are gone. He pushes me back against the apartment door. I feel it click shut behind me.

He takes my hands and brings my arms above my head, pinning my wrists together in the long fingers of one hand. His free hand blazes a fiery trail down my side, his thumb grazing my already-aching nipple, then on to my stomach, where it slips beneath the hem of my tank top.

He flattens his palm over my ribs and moves it around to my back and down into the waistband of my pants. The fit is loose there, so it's easy for him to slide into them, then down into my panties to cup my bare butt.

He pulls me against him, grinding his hips into mine as he sucks on my lower lip. "Do you know how hard it was to let you work tonight? To know that I can't touch you or kiss you or even watch you?" he pants against my open mouth. "All I could think about was what you look like naked and the little noises you make when I stick my tongue inside you."

His words make the lowest part of my belly fill with heat and tighten. He releases my wrists, but rather than push him away, I thread my fingers into his hair and crush my lips to his. I feel him working at the button and zipper of my jeans, and excitement floods me.

"It's only been a few hours and all I can think about is the way you taste, the way you feel wrapped around me. When you're so hot and so ready. So wet," he murmurs against my mouth.

Just as my need rises to fever pitch, a voice interrupts us.

"Nash?" It's my cousin Marissa and she's pounding on the interior garage door. Cash drags his lips away from mine and places his finger over my mouth to hush me. "Nash?" She bangs again. "I know you're in there. The garage is open and your car is here."

I hear Cash growl. "Shit! What the hell is she doing back?" he whispers.

My mind races. Although I know Cash and Nash are the same person—that Cash has been posing as both of them since his identical twin brother died—the fact that Marissa *doesn't* could pose a problem in instances like this, especially when she doesn't know about Cash and me.

"What should we do? We can't let her find out like this!"

Cash sighs and leans back to run his fingers through his mussed hair. Luckily, his preferred style is kind of spiky and disheveled, so it's not noticeable that my fingers have been in it.

My body aches with want, but my mind is already in gear for reality.

"Well, I guess the only thing to do is pretend like you're closing up. I'll think of something to tell her about Nash."

"Okay," I say, straightening my clothes and hair.

"I could kick myself for opening the garage door so early. I was gonna pull your car in after Taryn left." He sighs again and shakes his head slightly. When he looks back at me, his eyes are smoky and hot. "We're far from finished, though," he promises, leaning in and lightly biting my shoulder. A bolt of electricity shoots through me and lands between my legs. He knows exactly what to do and what to say to tear me up.

Dammit.

TWO

Cash

It takes everything I have to let Olivia go so I can answer Marissa at the door. Being with Olivia is like escaping into a bubble of perfection, into a bubble of life away from all the trouble and deception and . . . dirt of my double existence. And it's hard as hell to come back out.

I run my fingers through my hair again. My hard-on isn't a problem anymore; the sound of Marissa's voice took care of that. In fact, it almost gave me a damned vagina.

Gritting my teeth, I stomp to the door that leads out to the garage. I jerk it open, making no bones about my displeasure. Marissa's knuckles almost hit my nose; she was in the process of knocking again.

"Oh," she says, jumping back, evidently startled by my sudden appearance. She clears her throat. "Cash. Sorry to be so persistent, but I need to see your brother. Now. He won't return my calls and he owes me an explanation."

The longer she talks, the madder she gets. I can hear it in the pitch of her voice and I can see it in the thin line of her lips.

"Sorry, Marissa. He's not here. He left his car here last night and hasn't been by to pick it up yet."

"Why would he do that? Where was he going?" she asks, clearly puzzled.

"He didn't say. He just asked if he could leave it here for a day or two. That's all I know."

A sigh puffs out her cheeks. It's unlike Marissa to get so upset, to get so emotional. Normally her settings don't vary much. She goes from bitch to cold to lukewarm and back again. There's very little else to her personality.

"I guess I'll just keep trying his cell phone," she says, looking at his car. When she turns back to me, there is suspicion in her eyes. "I'll find him. One way or the other. Sorry to bother you, Cash." That's a lie. She's not the least bit sorry to bother me. And that threat? Oh, how I'd love to address it!

She starts to walk away, but stops and turns back. "Is Olivia still here? I saw her car out front."

"Yeah, she's closing up. Why?"

"I left her a couple of messages, but she hasn't called me back yet. I drove from the airport straight to Nash's and then came here."

"Do you want me to give her a message?"

She frowns and purses her lips as she thinks. "No, that's

okay. Just tell her I'll see her when she gets home. She shouldn't be much longer, right?"

I don't hit women. Ever. But, for about a tenth of a second, Marissa makes me wish I could. Not only is her interruption untimely, now she's going to screw up the rest of my night, too.

"Uh, no. She shouldn't be too much longer. You go on ahead. I'll give her the message and see that she gets out of here before too long."

Marissa's smile is cool and satisfied, which sets my teeth on edge. Being polite and unaffected, pretending I'm an uninvolved party, sucks ass!

"Okay. Thanks, Cash."

I smile tightly and wait until she turns away before I close the door. I'd really like to slam it and cuss a blue streak, but there's no point. Damn it.

Olivia is just putting the wraps on the liquor bottle pourers, the last task of every night, when I make my way out to her. She turns to look at me. For a fraction of a second, something feels different. Off. But then she smiles and I put it out of my mind.

That smile . . . Mmm, it makes my chest almost as tight as my jeans.

I walk over, stopping at the bar across from her. I watch as she wraps the last bottle and puts it back on the shelf. She looks around, making sure everything is done and the bar is clear before she turns to me.

"Have I ever told you how beautiful you are?"

Shyly, she looks away for a heartbeat before she brings her

eyes back to mine. She's still not quite comfortable with compliments, which shocks me. How someone who looks like she does could ever feel less than drop-dead gorgeous is beyond me. Yet she does. In a backward way, that makes her even more appealing.

"You might've mentioned it once or twice before," she says coyly, biting her lip in that way I love. It makes me want to carry her into the back room again. But it would have to be quick. And a quickie isn't what I want with this girl. Unless it can be followed up with something much more . . . thorough.

Watching me from the corner of her eye, she turns and starts walking slowly toward the cutout. With the bar between us, I walk with her.

"That's right. I did mention it before. I remember telling you how amazing you are. I think we were in front of a mirror." My dick twitches behind my zipper just thinking about sliding into Olivia from behind and coming inside her in the ladies' bathroom at Tad's bar. "Does that sound familiar?"

As she walks, she glances up at me from the corner of her eye. I see the flash of hot desire. I know she remembers it just as perfectly as I do.

She clears her throat. "Um, yeah. That seems vaguely familiar." Her grin is playful.

God, what a tease!

"Vaguely? Maybe I didn't pound it into you hard enough."

"Oh, I think you pounded it in plenty hard."

"Maybe I should've taken the time to give you a good tongue-lashing, too, then."

"Oh, I think the form of communication you used was very effective."

"So it's all coming back to you now?"

"Yes, it's all coming back to me."

"If you're lying, I could sweat it out of you, you know."

"I'm not lying. It's etched into my memory. Permanently."

"Maybe we should revisit it, just so you're clear on everything we discussed. I want to make sure it's in there. Nice and deep. So you never forget it."

Finally her grin turns into a giggle just as we're nearing the cutout at the end of the bar. When she rounds the corner, I'm there blocking her way with my body.

"I doubt there's anything you could do to get it in there any deeper."

"Oh, I can think of one or two things. The only way we'll know for sure, though, is to try. And I don't know about you, but I'm committed to this. Invested. And I'm nothing if not thorough."

I see something flicker in her eyes just before the light goes out and she seems to cool off. Before I can puzzle too long over it, she changes the subject.

"Oh! I nearly forgot. Marissa. What did she want?"

Again, I get the feeling that something's not quite right.

Apparently now's not the time to talk about what's bothering her. But I know something's up.

"Right. Marissa. She was looking for Nash. Obviously. She also wants to talk to you. Said she'd left you a couple of messages, but that she'll talk to you tonight. She's gonna wait up."

17

Either I'm crazy or there's a little relief in Olivia's expression.

"Yeah, my phone's in my purse. I haven't checked it yet. I guess I'd better get going, then. See what she wants. I mean, we can't blow this. It'd be a disaster if she found out about . . . you."

"Olivia, I told you I'd give up this charade of being Cash and Nash. I'm not sure I can help my dad anyway. And if that means—"

"Absolutely not! It's important, Cash! He's your father and he's in prison for killing your mother and brother, something he didn't do. No, you're not giving up anything. For me or for anybody else. We just have to be careful."

At least she's still saying "we" and counting herself as being involved. With me and everything else.

"You know I'd do it for you, though. To keep you safe."

"But I don't want you to do that. I'm perfectly safe. There's nothing to worry about. We'll just have to take things as they come."

I get the feeling there's a double entendre that I'm not quite getting. Yep. Something's definitely up with her.

"So, do you plan to tell Marissa about us, then?" she asks.

"That's up to you. Me? I don't care who knows, but I know *you* do. Especially the people around here."

"But you know why, right? I don't want to be the girl dating the boss."

"Yeah, I understand. That's why I stayed away most of the night. It's hard as hell to keep my hands off you. And my eyes. But I didn't want to make you uncomfortable."

Olivia's cheeks turn a pretty pink. "Really?'

"Really what?"

"You really can't keep your eyes off me?"

"God, for being so smart, you're thickheaded. Have I not made the way I feel about you abundantly clear?"

I thought I had, but maybe what's clear to me isn't so obvious to her. If that's the case, I'll have to make a point of being more . . . forthcoming.

Olivia shrugs and shifts her eyes to the side. I move in closer and bend until she looks at me.

"Hey, I know this is all new and I know how you feel about supposed bad boys like me." She starts to interrupt, but I stop her with a finger across her lips. "But I hope you're starting to see that there's more to me than you first thought. Than what you first assumed. You have to remember that I'm playing a part, too—two parts actually. A charade that would be even trickier if I didn't make each brother so extreme. You know that in some ways I'm both guys and in some ways I'm neither."

"How will I ever know the real you, then?"

I can see the worry in her eyes; I just don't know what has happened in the last little while to put it there. I thought we'd moved past all this.

I brush her satiny cheek with the backs of my fingers. "You already do. You'll just have to look past some of the behavior you see when we're around other people. I have to keep up appearances if you want me to go through with my plans."

She watches me closely. I'd love to know what's going through her mind, but I have a feeling that, in a thousand years, she'd never tell me.

Finally, she shakes her head.

"I still want you to go through with it. And I'll do my best to look . . . deeper than what I see. It just might take some getting used to."

"I understand that. This is not an easy thing, the life I lead. It's been my focus, all I've lived for the last seven years. But it's necessary."

"I know that. And I'm trying."

"That's all I ask."

An awkward silence slides between us and I hate it. I feel like there are things being left unsaid.

"I guess I need to get going, then. Back to the apartment."

Not only do I *not* want her to go, but I hate where things feel like they're at right now. I don't like unresolved issues. I've got enough of those in my life already.

"At least let me take you."

"That would seem strange when Marissa knows my car was here."

"Yeah, but more often than not, that P.O.S. won't even start."

"P.O.S.?"

"Piece of shit."

She grins. "Oh. Right. That's true."

"Just tell her it wouldn't start and I had to bring you home. If you want, I can go pull one of the spark plugs so it'll be true."

Her smile widens. "That sounds like an awful lot of trouble for li'l ol' me."

"Don't get a big head. I have ulterior motives."

"You do?" One eyebrow rises.

"Mmm-hmm," I say, winding my arms around her waist.

"And what might they be?"

"You'll just have to wait and see."

When I bend my head to hers, her lips feel warm and pliant, but not quite as responsive as I've come to expect. Something's still eating at her. I'll just have to keep at it until I figure out what it is.

I pull back and kiss her forehead. "Get your stuff. I'll meet you in the garage."

Rather than watching her go, I turn toward the front doors. I hate the feeling I get in the pit of my stomach just thinking about her walking away.

THREE

Olivia

The bike rumbles beneath me as I wind my arms tighter around Cash's waist. I must admit to feeling somewhat better about things after our conversation. I guess only time will eliminate the fear that I'm falling right back into the same trap with the same kind of guy. But if I've ever met a man that seems worth the risk, it's Cash.

I smile just thinking about him walking into the garage earlier, tossing one of my spark plugs into the air. He caught it, then winked at me as he stuck it in his pocket.

He went straight to his bike and climbed on. With a devilish grin and a shake of his head, he patted the seat behind him. "The lengths I go to just to get between your legs."

I laughed. I had no choice. His grin was so cute and engaging. So light and carefree. All the things I wanted to feel at that moment. Sometimes it's nice to be free of trouble and worry. Even for just a few minutes. And Cash gives me that. Often.

Now, I'm not at all pleased to see the familiar sights of my street come into view. I'm enjoying being close to Cash, feeling safe in his care. I don't want the ride to end.

But it does. Cash pulls up along the curb and rolls to a stop. I wait to see if he's going to flip down the kickstand. When he doesn't, I sigh and slide off the seat.

Cash watches me unbuckle the helmet from beneath my chin, pull it off, and hand it to him. He takes it, a small smile playing at the corners of his mouth. He doesn't move to put it on right away. I'm pretty sure he's thinking about the same thing I am—how to walk away without a kiss.

After all we've shared over the last few weeks, after all the words and kisses and nights and mornings, it seems so strange to just walk away like friends. In the pit of my stomach, it feels like a bad omen, that we'd part ways like this.

"Well, thank you," I say uncomfortably, trying not to fidget. Cash is frowning. I feel like frowning, too. "Um, I guess I'll see you tomorrow?"

"You're working your shift, right?"

I nod. "Yep."

"I'll call you in the morning. How 'bout that?"

"Sounds good." At least it's something.

The silence grows tense.

"I'll wait until you get inside. I don't know why Marissa didn't leave the lights on."

I glance behind me at the dark apartment windows. "Are

you really surprised by anything selfish and inconsiderate that she does?"

Cash's grin is small and wry. "I guess not. But damn!"

I sigh. "I know. But that's just the way she is. Some things never change."

Silence again.

"Okay, well, I'll talk to you tomorrow. Thanks for the ride. Have a good night."

"You, too."

I nod and rock back on my heels before I turn to walk up the sidewalk to the front door. I've made it only a few steps when Cash calls my name. I jerk around, anticipation curling in my stomach.

He can't stand it, either.

I walk quickly back to Cash. I feel more than a little deflated when he hands me my overnight bag, which he'd strapped to the back of the bike, behind the seat.

"Don't forget your bag."

I smile politely and take it from his fingers, turning once again toward the apartment. The anticipation in my gut cools into an uneasy sensation.

How can things have changed so much, so fast?

Taryn's comments, the memory of my mother's disapproving voice, and a whole slew of bad choices come crashing into my head like a rock slide.

I dig around in my purse for my key as I approach the front door. I'm distracted as I slip it in and unlock the knob, turning to wave to Cash. But he's not on his bike at the curb. It's resting on the kickstand, motor idling. He's charging up the sidewalk toward me. Before I can even blink, my back is pressed to the cool metal of the door, Cash's lips are on mine and his hands are in my hair.

I melt into him. Relief that he was feeling the same way battles for dominance with the desire to drag him into my bedroom, shut the door, and pretend nothing and no one exists outside it.

But before I can give in to that urge, Cash is pulling back, giving me room to breathe and giving rational thought the tiny crack it needs to wiggle back into my mind.

His eyes, darker than the night around us, search mine as his hands move from my hair to my shoulders and down my arms to grip mine. "Do me a favor," he whispers, curling my fingers over the back of his and bringing them to his mouth.

"What?"

His eyes never leave mine as he brushes his lips over my knuckles. "Dream of me tonight," he says softly. He watches me, waiting for a response. I have no words, so I simply nod. He doesn't need to know that no one else occupies my dreams. No one.

"Dream of my lips, teasing you." Straightening one of my fingers, he kisses the tip. His voice is like velvet and his words are like an aphrodisiac. "Dream of my tongue, tasting you." His tongue sneaks out to flick the end of my finger. A surge of desire rocks my core. "And I'll dream of you. Of what it feels like to be inside your warm, wet body." As if to show me what he feels, Cash sucks my finger into his mouth and pulls it in and out of his mouth, back and forth over his tongue. I can barely breathe.

He pulls it out, but before he lets it go, he gives it a gentle bite. I feel a burn in the pit of my stomach, a drop of lava in a boiling volcano.

"Good night, Olivia," he says quietly. And then he turns and walks away.

On legs that suddenly feel like jelly, I pivot toward the door. I focus with every ounce of my brainpower on putting him out of my mind before I do something stupid, like ask him to stay. I push open the door and reach around to flip on the foyer light before waving back to Cash.

But what I see stops both thought and movement.

The narrow table next to the door is turned over and the lamp that sits atop it is broken. The plant stand at the corner of the living room is overturned and there's dirt and foliage all over the floor. Some pillows from the couch are scattered across the floor, two having been thrown all the way over to the door.

Marissa has been home fifteen minutes at most. What in the world could've happened in such a short amount of time?

A shiver of apprehension works its way down my spine. When fingers wind around my upper arm and jerk me backward, I open my mouth to scream, but a wide hand clamps over it before any sound emerges.

My heart springs into wild motion behind my ribs, and my mind races, going back through every possible memory for any self-defense know-how. All I can think of, though, is *Aim for the balls! Aim for the balls!*

"Shhhh," a familiar voice hisses at my ear.

I calm immediately. It's Cash. It's Cash who's behind me, Cash who's holding me.

He releases me and steps in front of me, pulling me up against his back. "Stay close," he whispers from over his shoulder.

They'll have to peel me off your ass, mister!

All my senses are heightened by fear. The deep rumble of Cash's bike purring at the curb is an eerie backdrop for the absolute silence in the apartment. There are no other sounds. Not even those of Marissa.

Slowly, we make our way to the edge of the living room. Hyperalert, I look around, taking in even the tiniest of details. I see more signs of struggle—the lopsided position of the expensive clock on the wall, a small hole in the plaster not far from it.

I barely control a reflexive yelp when Cash's phone rings. I hear him growl as he fumbles for it in his pocket. He glances at the screen and then starts backing up, pushing me toward the front door.

He holds up his phone and I see the name on the Caller ID. My heart does a nervous little flip.

It reads *Marissa*.

"Hello," he answers quietly.

Without saying another word, Cash listens for a few seconds, then lowers the phone and sticks it back in his pocket.

"What? Why'd you hang up? What did she say?"

"It wasn't Marissa. Come on, we've gotta get out of here."

"Who was it, then? Cash, what's going on?"

"I'll tell you when I get you someplace safe."

With that, he practically drags me back to his bike and shoves the helmet at me. I bite my tongue and push the helmet onto my head before I climb on behind Cash.

Just before we take off, though, I change my mind.

He's not going to keep me in the dark about this. Either we share everything or this has to end now.

"No," I say as I start to climb right back off the bike. Cash straightens one arm in front of me to stop me. "Tell me right now what's going on or I'm getting off this bike."

In profile, there's enough light that I can see Cash's lips thin in irritation, but I don't let that intimidate me. My resolve has already hardened, like a thick icy shell.

I lean back and cross my arms over my chest.

"Fine," he snaps. "They've taken Marissa as leverage."

I gasp. "Who's they? And leverage for what?"

"The *Bratva*. Russian mafia. And they've taken her as leverage for the books."

"The books? Those accounting ledgers? I thought no one knew you had them."

"They didn't."

"Then how did they find out?"

"The only thing I can figure is that they have an inside man at the prison, maybe someone who can listen in on my conversations with Dad. We've been careful, but . . . if they've been listening long enough, they could put the pieces together. It wouldn't be hard for them to figure out that I plan to use the books to get their asses thrown in prison. And this last time I went to visit Dad, I mentioned that I'd told someone."

"Oh my God! But why on earth would they take Marissa, then?"

His pause makes me even more anxious. "I don't think they meant to take Marissa."

When the meaning behind his words sinks in, the bottom drops out of my stomach. "What?" I breathe.

"If they've been listening or watching very long at all, they likely know who I am. They called *my* phone, Cash's phone, to tell me about Marissa. If they didn't know I'm the same person, they'd have called Nash's phone, since he's her ex-boyfriend. Both of our numbers are programmed into her phone."

"So then, if they know who you are, why take Marissa?"

"They probably knew Marissa was away on a trip. And they thought you would be the only one coming back here. But when she showed up instead, they took her anyway to make a point."

"Which is?"

"That they could get to you if they wanted," he says quietly. "And that they know I'm Cash and Nash."

My guts swim with nausea. And fear. Both for Marissa and for myself.

I fight back tears. "But why would they want either of us? We don't know *anything*."

"It's not what you know. At least not entirely, I don't think. It's who you are."

"That would make sense with Marissa. She's the successful, influential one. The one who comes from money. I'm a nobody, from nowhere."

Cash turns around until he's looking into my eyes.

"Not to me, you're not."

Above the fear that's clogging my chest, I feel a little thrill at his words.

"They—"

"Baby," Cash begins, interrupting me. "I know you have questions, but right now I don't have all the answers. And we *have to* get out of here. Just hold that thought. Let me get us someplace safe and we'll talk more."

He doesn't wait around for my answer. He guns the engine and the motorcycle shoots forward, leaving me clinging to his back for dear life.

FOUR

Cash

It makes me feel both reassured and guilty when Olivia's grip tightens around my waist. I'm so glad I waited around for her to get safely inside. If I'd been just a few minutes earlier dropping her off or if she'd driven home by herself . . .

The air cools the cold sweat that pops out across my forehead.

I release the handlebars long enough to reach down and brush my fingers across the back of her hand. I want her to know that I *know* how scary this all is and that I'm *here*. In fact, I'm the reason she's even in any danger, which is where the guilt comes from.

If I hadn't taken such an interest in her, if I'd left it at just a fling, like all the others, no one would think to threaten her to get to me. By caring for her, I messed up. Now they're on to me and, as a result, on to Olivia.

I wouldn't wish anything bad on Marissa. I mean, she's a cold bitch, but she doesn't deserve to die because of it. And I'm sure that's what they have planned for her. What they had planned for Olivia.

The thought makes my stomach clench.

I speed up. My only concern right now is getting her someplace safe. And then I can work out the rest. I don't have a contingency plan for this; after all this time, I never thought they'd find out I have the books. Not until it was too late for them to do anything about it.

But I'm a smart guy. And my dad's got real experience with these kinds of people. We'll figure out something. We have to. It's that simple.

I take the most convoluted path I can think of to get downtown to the hotel I've got in mind. I check my mirrors constantly for lights or any other sign that someone's following us. I can't take anything for granted now.

When I pull up to the extravagant front entrance of the hotel, the valet appears. He's young and looks eager to drive my motorcycle.

After we're off, I tip him and watch as he drives the bike into the gated, underground parking area. I figure, if we weren't followed, my ride won't be easily discovered there. I'll take as many precautions as I can think of.

I grab Olivia's hand, leading her into the luxurious lobby of the hotel. Holing up here with her will cost me a pretty penny, but she's worth every cent. Besides, she might never have had the opportunity to stay at a place like this before. If I can manage to make her feel safe enough, she might actually enjoy it. The fact that I get her all to myself, in surroundings like this, for an indefinite amount of time is a huge bonus for me.

There's a brunette behind the reception desk. "May I help you?"

"We're just passing through. No reservations. Do you have any suites available for the week?"

"A suite? Of course, sir. Let me check availability for those dates."

As she types on her computer, I glance down at Olivia. She looks like she's holding up pretty well, all things considered. She's a little pale, but I'm sure she's scared shitless, so that's to be expected.

She looks up at me and smiles. It's a small, tight smile, but a smile nonetheless. I'll take it.

I squeeze her hand and bend to kiss her cheek. Before I straighten, I whisper in her ear, "I promise I won't let anything happen to you."

When I lean back and look into her big, green eyes, they're shimmering with unshed tears. Her chin trembles and my heart squeezes in my chest.

I've done this to her.

I don't know if it's fear for herself or Marissa's safety, or just the shock of what's happened on top of everything else that's happened in her life lately, but something is overwhelming her. I can see it and I feel responsible.

She squeezes my hand back. I take that as a good sign that maybe she doesn't completely blame me. Well, maybe that she doesn't completely *hate* me. Because the blame, no doubt, falls to me.

"Sir, we do have a suite available through next weekend. Do you have a rewards card with us?"

"No."

"Yes, sir. I'll just need your driver's license and the credit card you'd like to use for payment."

I notice she doesn't mention a rate for the room. I suppose it's understood that when you ask for a suite at a hotel like this, it's going to be exorbitant. I hand her the card for Dual. It's listed under the name of the corporation that owns Dual, which is hidden behind a couple of other shell corporations, so no one should be able to track its usage. Also, I specify that I want the reservation under that same name, for billing and tax purposes. She nods her head in understanding.

For most people, that would seem completely reasonable. And she's no exception. Several times, I see her eyes flicker to Olivia. No doubt she thinks I'm a businessman having an illicit affair on the company dime. I don't care what she thinks, though, as long as it's nowhere near the truth.

"Here are your keys, sir. Your suite is on the fifteenth floor. Suite elevators are just behind the water wall. Wave your key in front of the infrared eye once the elevator doors close. It will take you to your floor. Your room will be to your left as you exit the elevator. If you have need of anything, my name is Angela. It would be my pleasure to assist you."

"Thank you, Angela. One question: do you offer twenty-four-hour room service?"

Yes, sir. In-room dining is available at any time to our suite guests."

"Fine. I think we're all set for the night, then."

"Yes, sir. Enjoy your stay."

After taking the keys and the packet of information Angela gives me, I put my hand in the small of Olivia's back and guide her to the elevators. Once we're inside, her silence continues. I don't try to urge her into conversation because I know she has only questions, questions about things we shouldn't be discussing in a public elevator.

When the car comes to a smooth stop and the doors open with a muted *whoosh*, I usher Olivia out and to the left. I open the suite door and let her precede me into the room.

I can tell by her expression she's never seen accommodations like these before. Despite her shock and fear, she's still clearly impressed. And the suite they gave us is pretty upscale. It makes me happy I've got the money to treat her to something like this, even though the circumstances are less than desirable.

The first thing I notice when I walk through the door is the wall of floor-to-ceiling windows that look out over the impressive Atlanta skyline. They are the backdrop for the living room straight ahead, as well as the dining room to the left. Both rooms are done in a beige color and dark red. The lighting is soft, which has a soothing effect. As a guy, I totally approve.

There's a huge flat screen at one end of the living room and, beyond that, double doors that open to the bedroom.

I walk straight to the leather-bound hotel guide on the coffee table. Opening it to the menu, I hand it to Olivia.

"I'm sure you're hungry. Why don't you pick something to order from room service. I'll wait until they deliver it to leave."

"Leave? Where are you going?"

"Someone will be calling me back in another forty minutes. I want to be at the club when they do, just in case they can track my GPS. After the call, I'll get us burner phones to use until I can get this taken care of."

"Taken care of? Cash, tell me what's going on."

I sigh. And I think again, *Damn, I hate that I dragged her into all this. If I could've just stayed away from her* . . .

"They've got Marissa. They want me to bring the books. They're going to call back one hour from the first call."

"You can't take them the books by yourself, Cash. They'll kill you both! You need to call the police. My uncle is a very influential man. He'll have people moving heaven and earth to get his daughter back."

"Which is why he can never know. Until it's over, that is. It'll be a greater risk to her if we draw attention to it. They'll have more reason to clean up their mess. If I can get this done quietly, get Marissa back, I can figure out a new plan."

"You're going in there alone? To give them what they want, and then you expect them to let you go? And take Marissa with you? Cash, I don't even know these people, but I *know* that's not what they'll do. Criminals don't work like that."

I want to grin at her. *Like she has a lot of experience with criminals. Ha!* No doubt, this is all based on some classic mobster movies.

"Olivia, my father knows these people. Better than anyone. I'm not doing anything until I can talk to him. The books are hidden. I'm gonna tell them that they're in a safety-deposit box and that I can't get to them until Monday when the banks open. I would've already told them that, but I didn't have a chance. They said they had Marissa, to go get the books, and they'd call me in an hour with a place to meet."

"So, you're gonna leave Marissa with them until Monday?"

The look in her eye plainly says she thinks that's something a monster would do.

Flattening the binder up against her chest, I step closer to her and cup her cheek with my palm. "If I had any other choice, I wouldn't do this. But I don't. I *need* time. They won't do anything to her until they get what they want. And I have to be damn sure I've got my ducks in a row before I give them the only leverage I have."

She searches my eyes. And I let her. I know she has trust issues, anyway, thinking I'm the bad boy through and through. The reality of my situation only makes things that much worse. If she can just stick with me a little while longer . . .

"Can you trust me? Please! I know I've not given you many reasons to, but this one time, just go with your heart. I promise you, *promise you*, I won't let you down."

Even as I say the words, I know there's no way I can make a promise like that. But what I *can* promise is that, if I do, it

39

won't be because I didn't do everything in my power to live up to being the kind of guy she deserves. I want to be worth the risk. I want her to finally fall for the *right* guy.

She says nothing, only nods. I know it's hard for her, but the fact that she's willing to try gives me hope. Maybe bringing some familiar things will help ease her mind. I know she dropped her bag just inside the door of her apartment, and I didn't pick it up as we were leaving. I'll go by and get it on my way back. Maybe that will make her feel better. But then again, I'm a guy. What the hell do I know?

"Tell me what you want to eat. I'll order it. When it gets here, you can eat while I'm out. I'll go by your place and get your bag and some more clothes, and lock up. Is there anything specific you need?"

She pauses to think and then shakes her head. I'm not sure why she's so quiet, but I don't want to push her.

"Also, I'll need your cell phone. I'll take it to the club and leave it in the back, just in case. Until then, you can use one of the disposable phones I bring back for us. Okay?"

She nods again. If I know Olivia, she'll be worried about her dad and her best friend slash ex-fellow bartender, Ginger, not being able to reach her.

"You can call your dad and Ginger in the morning. Just tell them your phone's out of commission for a few days and that you'll be calling to check on them. We'll throw that phone away after you talk to them and you can use another one to call later in the week."

Her smile is agreeable but very tight. "It'll be okay. I'll *make it* okay."

She nods again, but still she doesn't speak. I refuse to acknowledge the possibility that I may already have screwed things up beyond repair. No, I'll just have to find a way to make her trust me, to get us out of this. Maybe then . . .

FIVE

Olivia

I can't even remember the name of my meal. Something fancy and exotic and foreign that I've never heard of. The only thing I care about is that it's chicken. I like chicken. And this is great chicken. My taste buds are working well enough for me to be sure of that. But I don't really taste it. Or maybe it's that I don't really enjoy it. My mind and my heart are too troubled and heavy to enjoy much of anything.

What in the world have I done? Not only did I do *exactly* what I knew I shouldn't—get involved with *another* bad boy—but I went and picked one who actually has a dangerous past. He's not just dangerous to my heart; he's dangerous *period*!

Obviously, running at this juncture is completely out of the question. It's not safe. Well, not for my physical well-being. It might be safest for my heart. But then again, maybe not. Even after all this, I still don't know what to make of Cash. Sometimes he's so sweet and sincere and . . .

He treats me like I'm something important. He talks to me like I'm something different. Not like I'm the throwaway kind he's used to loving and leaving. He seems to value me—my safety, my happiness. Just . . . me.

But I've talked myself into believing that before, into seeing what wasn't really there. On the one hand, I know better than to take the chance. I know from long experience what the wild ones do to girls like me. But on the other hand, something tells me to take the risk. A voice I've never heard before, one that seems to speak from somewhere inside my *soul*, tells me Cash is different.

The question is: What to do? What to do, what to do? That's always the question. And it's so much harder when everything's left up to me, when I'm the one forced to make the tough call, the tough decisions.

But right now, these circumstances are dictating my actions. I'm stuck. For the moment, anyway. I need to stick with Cash until all this mob stuff is resolved, which hopefully will be very soon. And then I can decide. Then I can *think*.

After I finish part of my meal, I get up and wander restlessly through the room. I don't like not having a phone, not knowing what's going on. I don't like not knowing if I'll ever see Cash again, if Marissa will be okay, if a raccoon has made its way into my apartment through my wide-open door and torn everything to shreds.

Yes, my mind works in very strange and nonsensical ways. I think it's so overwhelmed, it keeps coming back to whether the front door was left open. Like a broken record, it skips back to that over and over and over again.

I'm sure it probably was. I mean, I was a little distracted. To say the least. Maybe Cash closed it and I just wasn't paying attention. Maybe I closed it out of habit and just don't remember it. Or maybe neither of us did, and everything I've ever owned is in some homeless person's shopping cart. Who knows? I guess time will tell.

And if that happens to be the case, some stuff ought to be fairly easy to find. A homeless person who has recently redecorated their cardboard box with a two-thousand-dollar clock might stand out a tad, as would one walking the streets in Jimmy Choo shoes and a Prada evening gown. Of course, who'd want any of it back at that point? Not me! I say happy trails and I hope you enjoy Marissa's expensive thongs.

The only thing I could identify would be my Tad's Bar shirts. How sad is that? Maybe I ought to have my underwear monogrammed from now on . . .

I snicker and roll my eyes at my own wayward thoughts. I have very strange coping mechanisms.

The posh bathroom in our suite has a deep marble tub surrounded by all sorts of bathing accoutrements. On the back of the door hangs a thick robe. Although I have no clean clothes and no toiletries, a bath is too tempting to resist, so I turn on the spigot and undress as the spacious room fills with steam.

Thirty minutes later, I'm examining my pruned fingertips, thinking it's probably time to get out of the tub. The scent of the lavender bath products has permeated my skin and, after this long a soak, may very well have invaded my liver. But it's been worth it. The hot water seems to have drowned out a portion of my thoughts and worries. At least for the moment. My utter exhaustion has helped a fair amount, too. It's been a seriously long and emotionally taxing week!

I release the drain and let the water out of the tub, toweling off and wrapping myself in the soft, warm robe.

The rich sure do have it easy!

But I rescind that thought almost immediately. Cash comes from money, albeit the ill-gotten kind, and he might argue that some riches aren't worth the price. In fact, I'd guarantee he would. He's lost so much because of his father's pursuit of wealth. Granted, it began as an effort just to feed his family, but it soon turned into more than that. Yes, he wanted out, but he still benefited financially from his ties to organized crime. And look at them now—suffering on every front!

I make my way into the bedroom and slide under the covers to rest my eyes until Cash gets back. I push the worry over how long he's been gone to the very back of my mind. I refuse to think of him getting hurt, of what that would feel like and how it would affect my life. I can't think in those terms. I won't. Whether Cash and I have a future is one thing. Whether he'll break my heart is one thing. But his death? That's something else entirely. I can't bear the thought of a world without him in it, even if he's not mine.

I sit straight up in the bed when I hear a noise. My mind is instantly alert. I'm shocked that I managed to fall asleep. That's a testament to how fatigued I really was.

I see a shadow pass through the living room; I left the lights on in there. My heart thuds almost painfully against my ribs as I wait and listen. I hear the soft fall of footsteps against the hardwood floors and I look wildly around the room for some kind of weapon. The only things I can spot are a vase on the dresser that I could crack over someone's head and a hotel pen on top of the bedside table I could use to stab someone in the eye. A Bible no doubt resides in the top drawer, although I'm not sure I could really harm someone with that. God absolutely could, but I don't think he works on demand like that.

A presence fills the doorway and my heart jumps up into my throat. Within a fraction of a second, however, recognition calms me.

"I didn't mean to scare you," Cash says quietly from across the room.

I reach over to turn on the lamp, but he stops me. "Don't. I want you to be able to go back to sleep."

Fat chance of that happening! I think dryly, but as tired as I still feel, maybe there *is* a chance.

My pulse is just starting to return to normal when Cash turns to the side, reaches for the hem of his shirt, and pulls it over his head. The light from the next room gives him a gilded outline that highlights every rippling muscle as he moves and shifts this way and that to throw his shirt onto a nearby chair.

Blood sings through my veins and throbs in my chest when he reaches for his belt. He says nothing as he unbuttons and unzips his pants. I hold my breath when he pauses with his fingers in the waistband. I see his legs move as he kicks off his shoes.

I'm mesmerized. I can't help but watch him flick the material down his muscular legs and then step out of it. My heart stops and my mouth goes dry when I see that he's not wearing underwear. And he's hard. My mouth is the only thing on my body that's dry, though. My skin feels dewy, and warm moisture is gathering between my thighs.

Breathlessly, I watch him drape his jeans over the back of the chair and turn to walk to the bed, folding back the covers and sliding in next to me.

I don't move a muscle. And, at first, neither does he. After a minute, he reaches for me. The touch of his fingers sliding over my exposed forearm is like pure electricity. It brings chills out on my skin. They race up my arms and down my back and cause my nipples to furl into tight, aching buds.

I'm surprised and a little disappointed when he urges me onto my side. He pulls me tight against the curve of his body and spoons me from behind.

I can feel every rock-hard inch of him pressing into my backside, even through the material of the robe. Before I can even think about the wisdom of it, I wiggle my butt against him. It's instinct. And desire. My body's got a mind of its own, apparently.

I hear the breath hiss through Cash's gritted teeth and he grows absolutely still. For several long, tense seconds, he doesn't move. Neither do I. I want him to touch me, to put his hands and his mouth on me and make me forget the world exists, even for a little while. But when he finally does—touch me, that is—it's to drape his arm over my waist and tuck his fingertips against the bed, under my side. I feel his lips as he nuzzles my neck, and my heart melts right inside my chest.

He wants me. I can still feel it. But he's keeping himself in check for me, for my comfort and my emotional stability. His thoughtfulness pushes me one step closer to never being able to recover from having him in my life, from having met him and known the depth of feeling that I have for him.

For the umpteenth time since meeting Cash, I realize I'm quite possibly in big, big trouble.

Dammit.

We lie quietly together, breathing deeply and evenly, both of us waiting for our bodies to cool. I never thought it could be literally painful to be near someone. But it is. I ache with want, with *need*. There's a place, an emptiness that only Cash can fill. It's physical, yes. Oh boy, is it physical! Just the thought of him penetrating me, thrusting so hard and so deep inside me . . .

I squeeze my eyes shut and banish the thoughts from my mind. I have to start cooling off all over again.

Grrrrr.

But there's something more profound about the way Cash makes me feel, too. He fills an emptiness that has only recently become a gaping chasm in my soul. Since meeting Cash, in fact. It's like he created it, but at the same time, he can fill it, too.

With a heartfelt sigh, I turn off that brain channel as well. It's going nowhere good. Fast.

"So," I begin when the silence and the closeness is too much. "How'd it go?"

I chastise myself. The call is what I should be worried most about, anyway, not trying to keep my hands to myself. Or wishing Cash *weren't* keeping *his* hands to himself.

Cash's sigh stirs the hair behind my ear and gives me chills down one arm.

"They went for it. I don't think they liked it very much, but I think I kept my cool and convinced them that the books were locked up at the bank for safekeeping. Assholes," he whispers at the end.

"Did they let you talk to Marissa?"

"Yeah."

"And? How was she?"

"I think there's a pretty good chance she'll actually kill *them* by accident. I feel kinda sorry for 'em."

I can't help but grin. "So she wasn't taking her . . . captivity well?"

"She seemed to be polite to them, but she chewed my ass. There's no question who she blames in this scenario. The good thing is, unless they tell her I'm both brothers, she can just blame me and not drag Nash and all his accomplishments through the mud."

"With Marissa, I would expect nothing less."

I feel bad speaking that way about her when she's being held hostage. I mean, what a nightmare! But Marissa's pretty much a nightmare, too. Maybe the whole thing will somehow make her a better person. Or maybe a sharp blow to the head will give her an epiphany. Or maybe they used chloroform on her and it will alter her personality and make her likable and decent. Anything's possible, right?

"So what's the plan, then?"

"There are some things I need to look into tomorrow. And I want to go see Dad. Not only does he need to know about this, but he might be able to help."

"How? The man is in prison."

"I know that," Cash replies a bit sharply. "But he knows these people, knows how they think. Plus, he's always been good with plans and strategy. I don't want to risk overlooking something. There's too much at stake," he says, pulling me tighter against him.

We fall silent. I'm sure Cash's mind is churning harder and faster than mine, which is pretty damn hard and fast. But he has the added weight of guilt, not to mention all the buried pain this must be unearthing.

"Cash," I begin softly.

"Yeah, baby," he whispers near my ear, the endearment settling around me like a warm blanket.

"I don't blame you."

He squeezes me and presses his lips to my shoulder. I can barely feel them through the lapel of my robe.

"Can I take this off you?" he breathes. "I want to feel your skin against mine."

A pang of desire zings through me at the thought of him holding my naked body against his. It was only a few hours ago that we had sex for the fifth time today, but it feels like an eternity ago. So much has happened since then, so many emotions have come and gone, that it feels . . . different.

"Yes," I whisper in response, answering him before my mind can talk me out of it.

I start to sit up, but Cash stops me. He leans up on one elbow and pulls my hair away from my face and neck, bending to press his lips against the soft skin beneath my ear.

"Let me."

I do my best to relax when I feel his hand go to the knotted belt at my waist. He works it loose with his nimble fingers and then slowly pulls one end until it falls away.

Next, I feel his skin brush mine at my chest. He runs his hand along the inside of the lapel of the robe, opening it and pulling it away from my body all the way to my hip.

As light as the lavender scent emanating from my pores, Cash reaches up and eases the plush material over the rise of my shoulder, gently pressing his lips to the skin there. "You smell so good."

Ever so slightly, his hips tip into mine. Desire gushes low into my belly when I feel his hardness press against me.

He drags his fingers along the skin of my arm, pushing the robe away as he goes. I bend my elbow and pull my arm free of the sleeve. Cash reaches down to push the rest of it off my legs.

"Turn toward me."

Excitement humming along my nerve ends, I do as he asks and I turn onto my back and then continue rolling until I'm facing him. I'm so close, if I puckered my lips just right, I could kiss his chin.

In the dimly lit room, I can see his eyes sparkle like black diamonds. The light from the living room spills softly through the door and illuminates half his face, leaving the other half in deep shadow.

I can hear his breathing. I can feel the heat pouring from his body. I know he's as excited as I am, that he wants this just as much as I do, and yet he's willing to hold off. Just for me.

But what if I don't want him to? What if, despite the never-ending doubts and misgivings and horrors of the day, I want him? Is that enough? For now? Would that be so bad?

It is in a way. In another way, it's not. But the fact of the matter is, right now I need Cash. I need him to hold me, to kiss me, to touch me. I need him inside me, filling me up with his presence and his security. Tomorrow will bring new worries. I can think more then.

Just as slowly, Cash runs his fingers up over my collarbone and pushes the material off my other shoulder. It hangs on the tip of my breast and I see his eyes drop to my chest. I suck in a breath and hold it. His gaze burns like a physical touch.

Deliberately, he raises his hand to the center of my chest and runs the backs of his fingers over my nipple, freeing the robe and exposing my flesh to his hungry eyes. Again, he doesn't move for several seconds. Again, neither do I. When his eyes flicker up to mine, they're full of all sorts of things, but most apparent is resolve. He won't let himself give in. Not tonight. It's that important to him. Why, I don't know. Maybe *I'm* that important to him. I can only hope.

Leaning slightly forward, Cash pushes the robe off me, toward my back, running his hand over my butt and then up to the side of my thigh. When I'm lying in front of him, as naked as he is, he lets his eyes wander over me.

I see them close just before he rolls onto his back and raises his arm to loop over my head. He pulls me onto his chest. I let my hand skate over the hard muscles of his stomach and drape my knee over his thigh.

I can't hear him breathing. I wonder if he's holding his breath. I don't know, but I can hear his heart slamming against his ribs. He's fighting me, fighting us, fighting *this*.

I think for a second of teasing him a little, of changing his mind, but respect for what he's doing rears up and stops me. I don't want to make more out of his consideration than what it is, but that still leaves me with the question: what does it mean?

Cash's lips graze my hair just before he croaks, "Go to sleep, baby. You're safe. I promise."

On some level, I must believe him. So I sleep.

Something shifts at my back. It's smooth and warm, and it takes me less than a second to realize it's Cash. He's behind me. And he's naked.

His hips flex, pressing his erection into the crease of my butt. Without thought to consequence, I arch my back and push into him.

I hear him suck in a breath and my stomach flutters in response.

He's awake.

Please don't let this be a dream.

One big hand skates over my hip and onto my stomach, then up to cup my breast. With his fingertips, he teases the nipple until it aches for him, for his mouth. Reaching up, I place my hand over his, squeezing his fingers. He kneads my sensitive flesh until my pulse steps up to a quicker beat.

I feel his lips at the curve of my neck. Then his tongue. It sneaks out to wet a circle on my skin, and then he nips it with his teeth. Chills break out down my chest and back, and my belly tightens in anticipation.

I want this to happen. I need this to happen. So I go with it. I encourage it. I throw myself into it.

Reaching behind me, I grab his hip and pull him into me, grinding my butt against him. I hear him groan as his hand leaves my breast to travel back down my stomach to the juncture of my thighs. I spread them the tiniest bit to allow him to touch me. And he does. He slides one long finger between my folds, pausing only briefly to flutter over the nub at the top before slipping inside me.

"Mmm, what's this?" he says, pulling his finger out and then thrusting it in farther. My nails bite into his hip and he flexes against me again. He's even harder. And bigger. If that's possible.

"Were you dreaming about me?" he whispers in my ear. "It sure feels like you were." He rubs me with his palm and penetrates me with his fingers. "Were you dreaming of me touching you like this? Or were you dreaming of me doing more?"

I say nothing. I can't think past what he's doing to me, past what I *want* him to do to me. Over and over and over again.

"I think you were. I think you want this, but you're afraid. But not tonight. Don't be afraid tonight. Just let me have you. Let me show you how good we are together."

Gently, Cash moves from behind me. I start to roll onto my back, but he stops me. "No," he says flatly. When I start to speak, he cuts me off. "Shhh," he murmurs, rolling me onto my stomach. "Onto your knees." I hesitate only for a second, but it's long enough. "Do it," he orders softly. "I promise you'll like it."

I come up onto my hands and knees. I feel Cash's warm body at the backs of my legs and my butt as he moves in closer to me. His warm hands find my hips. His fingertips dig in and he pulls me back into him, his hardness pressing against me. A shiver of pure lust trembles through me.

Pushing gently, he urges me forward. I crawl toward the headboard until I'm hovering over my pillow. "Reach out with your hands."

I do it, curling my fingers around the top of the wooden headboard. Slowly, Cash bends over me until I can feel his chest against my back. He breathes into my ear, "Spread your legs." When I do, one of his hands moves between them from behind me. He puts his thumb inside me as his fingertips play with the slippery skin between my folds. If I were standing, I would collapse. I feel his touch all the way in my knees. I can't stop the moan that leaves my lips in a rush.

"You like that?" His tongue flicks my earlobe.

"Yes," I say with what little breath I have.

He moves my hair aside and kisses the back of my neck, then the center of my back. I feel his warmth moving away as his lips make a trail down to my lower back and over my butt.

The bed moves as he shifts behind me. I feel his head slip between my legs and press into the pillow between them. I look down just as he looks up and, in the low light, I see his black eyes sparkle. The fire in them is enough to make me flush all over.

He never takes his eyes off mine as he, from the back, winds his hands around the tops of my legs and pulls me down onto his mouth.

The first touch of his tongue is like lightning. Heat gushes through my core and lands in a puddle against his lips as they move over me.

"Ride me," he growls, his voice thick with desire. As if to encourage me, he thrusts his tongue deep inside me.

With his hands on my legs, he urges me into motion. In and out, his tongue moves within me. Back and forth I move on his tongue, rocking on my knees, sliding over his face. His lips and face stimulate all parts of me at once and it's nearly more than I can bear.

My breath comes in quick bursts. My fingernails dig into the wood of the headboard. My hips rise and fall over his mouth. My pulse races out of control.

Faster and harder I grind against him. When I hear his moan, it flips open the floodgates of pleasure and my world flies apart on the tip of his tongue.

He holds me to him as I close my eyes and give in to the spasms that rack my body. Before the contractions fade into blissful nothingness, I feel Cash move. Within seconds I feel him behind me. I feel his fingers probing me, gliding in and out of me. And then I feel something bigger.

His first quick thrust takes my breath. With a groan, he pulls out and slams into me again, renewing my orgasm.

Wave after wave, I feel my body squeezing tightly around him. I'm so full, so very, very full. I feel him everywhere, like he's penetrating all the way into my chest. Over and over, he withdraws his length and then drives it back into me, seating himself more deeply each time.

"Take it all, baby," he says through gritted teeth. The words are so hungry, so erotic, I cry out.

His rhythm increases and so does his breathing. I know what's coming. I know *he's* coming.

His body stiffens and he growls with the first pulse of his climax. He pounds into me in short strokes as he leans forward and twists one hand into my hair and buries his teeth in the skin of my shoulder. It doesn't hurt, doesn't break the skin; it only enhances the pleasure that's already flooding my body.

And just like that, I'm exploding all over again. Coming apart. Wrapped in Cash's arms. Holding him within my body.

Within my heart.

Within my soul.

SIX

Cash

Sundays are big visiting days at prisons. It's always sad to see the number of families sitting at the separated tables. Kids talking to fathers they barely know. Wives talking to husbands they barely see. Lives lived in a way that's barely human. In a place like this, it's easy to see that all mistakes, large and small, have consequences. The larger the mistake, the heftier the consequence. I just hope nothing I've done or have to do in the immediate future lands me in here. I think I'd rather be dead.

On autopilot, I go through the familiar motions of getting in to visit my father. I'm sitting behind the glass, my hands folded on the table in front of me, when they bring him in. Although I'm not aware of wearing any particularly telling expression, something I'm doing alerts my father.

He gets right to the point the instant he picks up the black phone on the wall. "What happened?"

I meet his concerned eyes, eyes just a shade or two lighter than mine, and I shake my head once, casually reaching up to tap my right ear with my fingertip. He watches me intently for several long seconds. I know he's processing it all and that contingency plans are being formulated as we speak. Or don't speak, as it were.

Finally, he nods. Just once, a short, curt bob of his head. He understands. I can see it in his eyes.

"Nothing happened. It's just been a long weekend. Work's been busy."

The conversation drifts to mundane topics, nothing that would be totally out of the ordinary for one of my visits. We catch up on people and events and daily real-life things, nothing worthy of any extra attention. I'm hoping it's just enough to lull any listeners into a lazy state of boredom.

Finally, Dad steers the conversation back to the most important thing. But, crafty guy that he is, he does it in such a way that it doesn't seem obvious. At least I *hope* it doesn't.

"So how'd that fishing trip go? Catch anything?"

I don't fish. Nash did, but I never have. Dad knows that. And that's how I know that we're not really talking about fishing.

"Nah, it was a no-go. Ended up spending the weekend hiding out. You know, to work."

He nods slowly, meaningfully. I know he picked up on my use of the term *hiding out*.

"It can be dangerous. To work too much."

"Yeah, I know it can be," I say, nodding for emphasis. Still he watches me closely. It's like we're carrying on a much deeper conversation without saying a word.

"Gonna have to hand over some of the important duties to someone else, I think." I hope he understands what I'm really going to have to hand over.

"Sometimes you have to do what you have to do, Cash. Things don't always turn out like we want. Or like we plan. Sometimes, you just have to go with it and do what you think is best. It's all about surviving this life."

"I feel like my hands are tied."

He nods again. "Well, giving up everything can have a whole different set of consequences. Do you have a plan B?"

I shake my head, raising my hand helplessly. "No, but I'm open to suggestions. I've still got time. Just not much. The club's in trouble." He scratches his chin, still watching me. "Anything you can think of that might help? Anything *else* I can do?"

"You're so damned stubborn," he murmurs. "You had to go all in, didn't you? With that club. And risk someday going down with the ship."

Before Dad got arrested, he didn't want me to have the mob's books, didn't want me involved. I convinced him that not only would they provide us with some leverage, but they would also keep me safe. As long as Dad's employers knew the books were . . . somewhere, they could never risk making a move until they confirmed who had them or where they were.

Only now they've confirmed the *who*.

"That's what I'm trying to avoid. Thought you might have some advice. You're a pretty smart old man, after all." I say this with a grin, a loving one. And Dad recognizes it. I see it in his eyes, all the affection I have for him reflected there.

"You need help at the club."

"I'm open to it. Any suggestions?"

"Here's what you do. Take out two ads in the paper."

"Does anyone still use an actual newspaper?" I tease.

"Some people do," he says with a casual shrug. In this case, *some people* must be pretty important people. "But there's an online place you can advertise, too. Don't put the second ad in there. Only the first one. You might get a quicker response from it."

He goes on to tell me exactly where to place the ads and how to word them. I make notes in the crappy burner phone I'm carrying.

"You should hear something in a few days. At the latest. Maybe getting some help around there will free you up a little more."

"Yeah. This is really becoming a problem for some of my employees, too."

He knows that Olivia bartends for me.

"Well, this might be the answer, then. Sometimes it takes drastic measures."

"I'm desperate. At this point, I'd be willing to try pretty much anything."

He nods again, but says nothing. In his eyes, I see regret.

Deep, painful regret and sorrow. Although he doesn't have the details, he knows that things are starting to go sideways. Coming to a head. And not in a good way, not in *our* way. Having to hand over the books was never part of the plan, never a consideration. After all this time, I never thought . . . well, I just never thought. And not thinking has cost me. And it might *keep* costing me.

Unless I can figure out something else. Maybe the ads and whomever they're signaling will be all the answer I need. I hope so.

As soon as I get back to my bike, I check my phone. The signal is lost completely inside the prison. Olivia knew I'd be unreachable during that time. She seemed fine with it, much more so than me. I rushed through the visit as much as I dared so I could get back out into the wired world. Now I've got four bars and no messages, which is a good thing. I guess. No emergencies. No reason to worry.

But I wouldn't have minded finding a text or a message from her, anyway, reason or not. Just to let me know she's okay. Or maybe that she missed me.

After a few seconds of internal debate, I give in to the urge and push the button to dial Olivia's temporary cell phone number. It's not that I have anything particular to say. I suppose it's just that, despite the fact that I've been gone only a couple of hours, I want to make sure she's okay. Just check in. It's the polite, considerate thing to do. That's all. Nothing more.

Just keep telling yourself that, buddy.

I roll my eyes at that voice in my head. He's a smartass.

"Hello?" comes the sleepy response.

"Did I wake you?"

"That's okay. I was just being lazy, but I need to get up. Where are you?"

"I'm still at the prison. I'm getting ready to leave. Just thought I'd check in."

"Really?" There's a smile in her voice. And a hint of something else. Pleasure, maybe? It seems like she's happy that I'm checking in with her.

"Does that surprise you?"

She pauses. "Maybe."

"Why?"

Another pause. "I don't know. I guess I just keep expecting you to . . ."

She trails off, but I have no problem finishing her thought. She still thinks I'm one of her typical bad-boy mistakes. Vaguely, I wonder if I'll ever be able to do enough or say enough or show her enough that I'm not like that. At least not in the ways that count. Or will she always compare me to them? If she does, she'll always find similarities. But will she see the differences? And will they be enough?

Sometimes it sounds like a battle I can't win. After living the lives of two separate people for all these years, after having to pretend to be two completely different guys—neither one the true me—what I really want is someone who sees the *real* me and accepts it. All of it. The good, the bad, and the ugly.

But that can't be my primary concern at the moment. There are too many more important things to worry about. Like keeping everyone alive and safe and unharmed. Even people I don't particularly care for, like Marissa. I couldn't live with something like her death on my conscience. Or even her being hurt. I already feel like shit about this whole mess and nothing has really happened. Just the thought of it escalating and, God forbid, ending badly gives me a little insight into what Dad must feel every single day. He has the death of my mother and brother on his hands, not to mention whatever else he's done during his employment with the Russian mafia.

Olivia clears her throat and brings me back to the present. "How'd it go?"

"I'll tell you all about it when I get there. Do you need anything as I come through town?"

"Ummm, not that I can think of. With what you brought last night, I think I'm all set."

"Good. Okay, I'll see you in a little while for lunch, then. We can order something up to the room."

Immediately, my thoughts go to the dining room table in the hotel room, to pushing aside china and crystal glasses and heavy silverware, to tearing that damned robe off her and easing my body into hers.

I bite my lip when I feel blood flow divert away from all my vital, thinking organs in favor of the fun ones. I've gotta stop thinking about shit like that. I can't very well ride back to Atlanta, on a motorcycle, with a huge hard-on. At least not comfortably.

"Mmmm, that sounds good." Part of what makes me bite my lip harder is what she said; it's like she knew exactly what I was thinking. But most of the reason is the *way* she said it. She's got the sexiest voice when she talks low like that. It's got a hoarseness to it, like a rumble that I can feel vibrate through me. Wakes my dick up every time. And he didn't need any help today!

"All right then. See you soon." I hang up. I know it probably seemed abrupt to her, but it was either that or take a few extra minutes to walk off a boner before traveling back to the city. And I hate leaving her alone for one second longer than I have to. I'm pretty sure she's safe, but I'm not *certain*. And as long as I can't be *certain*, I won't be taking any unnecessary chances.

SEVEN

Olivia

I flip my head up from drying my hair and stare at my reflection. I can see the worry in my eyes. I don't know if Cash can or not, and if that's making things worse, but something sure is.

It seems like the tension between us is growing. And not in a good way. The sexual tension is still there. For sure. But it's taking a backseat now to whatever else is going on to trouble the waters.

It might just be a collection of things. I know I'm feeling a little uncertain. About him, about the situation, about . . . everything.

Damn Taryn and her stupid comments!

I know I shouldn't pay that much attention to her, but it seems like her words snapped me out of a trance, one where I was ignoring everything in order to focus on Cash. And look where that got me! A kidnapped cousin and an all-expenses-paid trip to a luxury hotel that might as well be a prison.

It wouldn't feel so much like captivity if Cash and I weren't so tense around each other. I *know* what my issues are. It's his that concern me. Why has he grown distant and uneasy? Is it just the situation with Marissa? Does he feel guilty? Is he worried about giving up the books and losing the only means he had of helping his father? I'm sure he's feeling all those things. But the question is: Is there more? Does it have anything to do with me?

As I finish getting ready for work, I grumble silently over this strange new predicament and how selfish I am to be so focused on my relationship with Cash when there are more important things at stake. When I've threaded thin gold hoops through my pierced ears, I shut off the bathroom light and make my way to the living room.

"Okay. I'm ready whenever you are," I say to Cash where he's sitting on the couch, pretending to watch television. I can tell by the way he starts when I speak that his mind was elsewhere. Deep, deep, deep in elsewhere.

He smiles. And my heart skips a beat. Just like always.

"I guess it's working out perfectly that you wanted to work tonight, huh? Now we both have reason to be there. You can make some money and I can keep an eye on you."

"You don't have to keep an eye on me. In fact, we don't even need to stay here, probably. They have Marissa. You're taking them the books. This should all be over with tomorrow, right?"

I'm not sure what to make of Cash's expression. But even if I did, I wouldn't trust that I'm interpreting it correctly. I think I'm just too sensitive right now. To everything about him.

He nods and smiles, but the smile is tight. "It should be, yes. Just bear with me a little while longer. Please."

The last word is added with a hesitant sincerity that makes me feel bad for . . . something. Like I've wounded him somehow. But I can't imagine that's true. Still, it seems that way.

"Of course. Whatever you think is best. I mean, come on. Room service and marble bathtubs? What's not to love, right?"

"Precisely." His grin still doesn't reach his eyes.

"Let's go make some money."

Ten minutes later, as we zip through the streets of Atlanta on his bike, I revel in the feel of having my arms wrapped around Cash's waist. It's the one time I can hang on to him without giving thought as to why I'm holding on or if I'm holding on too tight. Or if I should be holding on at all.

I wish I had a giant rewind button. I'd take us back a few days, to the day he came to Salt Springs to find me, to the day I felt like I was his and he was mine, to the day I stopped thinking about everything else.

To before I talked to Taryn. And she reminded me that leopards don't often change their spots. They're beautiful as they are, but they should be admired from a distance. Where they can't reach you with their claws, claws that could easily tear a girl's heart out.

When Cash rounds the corner and Dual comes into view, my heart sinks. Taryn is already here. And she's sitting in her

71

car, no doubt waiting for someone to unlock the doors and let her in. I heard Cash call Gavin, the part-time manager, and tell him not to worry about opening up, that he'd be in.

Holy crap! I didn't even think about that!

As Cash drives past her car and around the building to his garage, I see her eyes follow us. Even through the tinted face shield of the helmet, I can feel the sharp tips of the daggers she's throwing my way. I assume that this will bring an abrupt and likely ugly end to our truce.

Dammit.

The garage door opens with the push of a button on Cash's bike and he guides us inside and cuts the engine. I hop off quickly, hoping Taryn doesn't come around and make a big scene.

"I'd better get in and get to work," I say, handing Cash my helmet. Slowly, he reaches out to take it from my hand, eyeing me suspiciously. After several uncomfortable seconds, just when I think he's going to make an issue of keeping our relationship (whatever it might actually be) from the others, he nods. I give him a quick smile and dart into the apartment, through the office, and out into the bar itself, stowing my purse safely behind the counter.

I waste no time getting to work, uncapping liquor bottles, making sure the coolers are stocked, and then setting about to slice lemons, limes, and oranges. I see Cash cross the room to unlock the doors, but rather than going back to his office, he goes outside. It's a good fifteen minutes before he comes back in. And the thing that irks me most? About sixty seconds after he comes in, Taryn finally makes her appearance.

And she's smiling.

Broadly.

Now what the hell does that mean?

The lump of nausea in the pit of my stomach tells me it means nothing good. At least not for me.

I blink away the tears that sting my eyes. How could I be so wrong? Again! It felt so right. I was so close.

Taryn starts to whistle as she gets her station set up. Whistle, for God's sake! Call me crazy, but I think she's gloating. Can whistling sound like gloating? Um, I'm pretty sure it can. And I'm pretty sure this does.

I grit my teeth and ignore her as best I can. I'm thankful when Cash turns on the music and it drowns out her obnoxious happiness. With a ruthlessness that feels like it's directly linked to my survival, I put every ounce of my focus into work. I can't stand to be inside my own head for one more second.

EIGHT

Cash

I get up and walk to the bookcase across from my desk for the third time. I've left my office door cracked so I can make sure Taryn is behaving herself.

When I went outside after unlocking the front doors, it was with the intention of admitting that Olivia and I are seeing each other and then giving Taryn an ultimatum. I didn't want her coming in and giving Olivia a hard time. But I think I underestimated just how big a role Taryn's ego would play. She beat me to the punch on being the first to speak and, in the process, gave me the perfect out. Olivia's secret is still safe.

"That girl really needs a new car," she said cheerfully, glancing back at Olivia's car as she walked across the parking lot toward me.

"She can't afford one right now. And you don't need to be

giving her shit. That girl's having it pretty rough. I feel sorry for her, and if you knew what all was going on in her life and with her family, you would, too. So do us all a favor and keep the claws in, okay?"

She stopped in front of me. Looking hard into my face, she stared for at least a minute or two before she said anything. Even now, I wonder if she was looking for the truth. And I wonder what she ended up finding.

Whatever it was, she never let on that she didn't believe me. She laughed and shook her head. "So what was it this time?"

"Spark plugs, I think."

"I guess I could start giving her a ride, since we'll be working the same shift for a while."

"Yeah, 'cause that wouldn't make her feel worse or anything," I said sarcastically.

"What? I can be nice."

"You *can* be, but you *haven't* been. That would be like rubbing salt in a wound if you offered her a ride to work because her car's a junker and she can't afford anything else right now. *Especially* after the way you've treated her."

I had to grit my teeth. Just thinking of Taryn mistreating Olivia was enough to make me see red. But I couldn't let her see that. So I hid it all behind the mask that my face has become.

"Are you kidding me? I bought her a shot last night and offered to take her out after work. What else do you want me to do? Donate my blood to help her pay for a car?"

"Don't be a smartass. I didn't ask you to be her best friend.

That's on you. I'm just telling you not to give her so much shit. She's having a tough time."

Taryn smiled in that vampy way she has, a way that used to end up with us getting naked somewhere but now does absolutely nothing for me. I hoped she saw that, but her next action assured me she didn't.

"Anything for you, boss." She leaned in toward me as she spoke. Not enough to rub up against me, but enough that her ample chest was just brushing mine.

"Now that's the attitude I like for my employees to have," I said nonchalantly, turning to head back into the bar.

I purposely didn't glance at Olivia on my way back in. I didn't want her to think I'd betrayed our secret. Well, it's not really our secret; I don't care who knows. It's more her secret.

Now, as I glance out at the bar, I see Taryn smiling and tending her customers. I haven't seen her antagonizing Olivia at all. Of course, I haven't really seen her pay much attention to her either way. I'd much prefer her to just ignore Olivia. That would be best all the way around.

I'm sitting down at my desk when my phone beeps, the notification of an incoming text message.

> Is this the number for help wanted in the twin cities?

My pulse picks up. It's a response to the ad.

> Yes.

My reply is short. I don't really know what else to say.

You're lucky I'm in town. I'll be there in 3 hours.

My first thought is to wonder how a perfect stranger would know where to find me. The only thing listed in the online ad other than my phone number was the short two-sentence blurb my father had me post: *Urgent help wanted in the Twin Cities. Stop.*

It says nothing of my location. Maybe the area code of my phone could be used to get a general location, but nothing specific enough to actually find me.

Unless there is tracing involved.

You know where I am?

The reply makes me uneasy.

Of course.

I've deduced that people from my father's past have been keeping an eye on us, but it seems like the group is much larger—and hopefully a lot friendlier, in some cases—than I'd originally suspected.

Of course, I have a thousand questions, things like *Who the hell are you? How are you associated with my father?* and *Why have you been watching me?* I'm torn between asking now or waiting. In the end, I figure it's best to wait. Dad had me reach out to them. I have to trust that he knows what he's doing. I know he'd never get me hurt if he could help it. Still, the whole thing makes me nervous.

Putting that out of my mind, I think about how grateful I am for technology. The online ad alerted somebody. Fast. Somebody my father thinks can help. And, judging by the short, gruff text, he's probably not the type of person most people would call a "pleasant" association. But that's the nature of the business my father was in. I've known it for a long time. I just never expected it to have such a profound and intimate impact on *my* life.

Pulling out the books for the club, I work on some accounting, hoping that will help me get through the next three hours. I can't really go out and mingle in the club—I can't keep my eyes off Olivia—so that leaves me stuck back here. Waiting.

Just over an hour later, something that's been niggling at the back of my mind rushes to the front. It's got its unpleasant aspects, which is probably why I haven't given it my full attention before now. It makes it seem like I don't trust my father. Which I do. But I guess I don't trust anyone one hundred percent, especially not with Olivia's safety hanging in the balance.

I pick up my phone and dial the one person I feel like I can trust with anything and who would do whatever he could to help me out in a pinch. In the absence of my real brother, he's stepped in to fill the void. He's the closest thing to family I have on the outside.

"Damn, you're needy!" comes the familiar voice of Gavin Gibson, my part-time bar manager and friend. His words still carry a little bit of a lilt from his childhood in Australia.

"This isn't about work, Gav. It's something else. I need your help."

There's a pause. When Gavin speaks again, all teasing is gone from his voice.

"Anything. You know that."

"Can you come to the club for a couple hours?"

"Uh, yeah," he says uncertainly. "Just let me take care of a couple things and I'll be right over. Give me forty-five minutes?"

"Sure. See you then."

After I hang up, I realize this was a good decision. I feel better about the situation already. I need my own people, people I can trust, people I know. Going into this alone would be crazy and irresponsible, even though my father's directing the traffic. Still, I need to cover all my bases. And Gavin can be my secret weapon.

NINE

Olivia

Plastering on a smile, I'm fighting to keep my disposition light for my customers. I hear what sounds like a battle cry from the other end of the bar and I glance down to see Taryn happily celebrating . . . something. When she turns to change the music, I know by the first few notes what's going on. Someone is getting a body shot.

Most of the crowd is familiar enough with Dual to know what the song means and what a body shot is, so they quickly scramble to Taryn's end of the bar to watch the entertainment. I think the only more effective way to clear out space in the room would be to start screaming, "Fight!" and point toward the door. The place would empty in four seconds flat.

The girl who will be receiving the body shot looks like the type that volunteers for them. A lot. I would be willing to bet she is made of eighty percent synthetic materials and that her clothes belong to her much smaller sister. The mass of white-blond hair atop her head completes the picture of a bimbo.

She wiggles and jiggles before she lies back onto the bar. I find it amusing that no one has to adjust her clothing at all for the shot. An ample amount of her stomach is already exposed by her outfit.

Taryn limes and salts her belly, and goes one step further by pouring the tequila into her navel, which only works for people with a fairly deep one.

Oh boy! Some guy is gonna love sucking that out!

I look into the drooling crowd for salivating idiot number one. He's easy to spot. He's all bright-eyed and bushy-tailed at the thought of licking something off this girl's body. All his friends are clapping him on the back and he's actually rubbing his hands together in anticipation.

Try to hold it together there, quick shooter.

I giggle at my thoughts. He's not so bad, but some of his friends look like they could be poster children for premature ejaculation. My bet is that a couple of them run off to the restrooms after they watch this little show.

Ack!

Since my customers are otherwise occupied, I use the time to wipe down my station, doing anything and everything I can to keep my mind on work. Periodically, I glance down at the commotion on Taryn's end. The crowd goes wild when the guy starts licking the salt off the girl's stomach. I shake my head and smile. It really doesn't take much to get this group fired up.

Just as my eyes are moving back to the task at hand, I see a shadow move in the sliver of light coming from Cash's office. My senses are attuned to that corner of the room, no matter what I'm doing or how hard I try to ignore it.

Cash is leaning up against the doorjamb, watching me. Even across the distance, I see the heat in his eyes. I *feel* it. He doesn't have to tell me what he's thinking. I know it as certainly as I can see it in the back of my mind. He's remembering the night this music played for us.

Like instant replay, the scene—the smells, the sights, the sounds, the feelings—unfolds in my mind with perfect clarity. A slow burn starts low in my belly as I think of Cash draped over me. It spreads like fire as I relive his lips and tongue traveling over my stomach, dipping into my navel and teasing the edge of my shirt.

I feel my pulse pick up when I remember the look in his eyes when he took the lime from my mouth. It's the same look I've seen there more than a dozen times since then. That's the way he looks when he watches me come. It's the way he looks when he's watching me undress. It's the way he looks now. It's a hungry look that says he wants me. Right this minute, with nothing between us but hot breath and damp skin, he wants me. Now.

And there's no denying that I want him, too. Just as badly.

The crowd between us cheers, but I don't look to see what's happening. I can't tear my eyes away from Cash. He's like the sun that my world revolves around—no matter how much I try to gravitate away from him, to set my heart and my body free of him, he draws me. Compellingly. Inexplicably. Undeniably.

He arches one brow and I feel desire shoot through me. It almost takes my breath.

Oh God, how I want him!

I've never wanted someone this way. So deeply. So completely. So desperately.

But that's the part that gets me into trouble. It's the part that scares me.

A group of guys moves away from the action, coming between us and breaking Cash's very disconcerting eye contact.

The moment is gone.

But not the effects.

Every day, every hour, every minute I spend in his presence, Cash is getting further and further, deeper and deeper under my skin.

"You must be Olivia," a lightly accented voice says, drawing my attention away from the door.

When my eyes make their way to the owner of the voice, I know my mouth drops open. If the earth holds anyone who ranks anywhere close to Cash in good looks, it would have to be this guy.

Holy furry crap balls! He's gorgeous!

A thick patch of jet-black hair—cut close and styled like Tom Cruise's hair in *Top Gun*—sits above a very tan face that is the picture of classic good looks. Wide brow, high cheekbones, straight nose, chiseled mouth, strong jaw—he's just a man's man. That's all there is to it. But it's his great smile and twinkling ocean-blue eyes that turn him from great-looking into gorgeous.

Even while I'm thinking this, while I'm cataloging his attributes, I'm aware of a lack of any flicker of excitement, any glimmer of attraction. He's handsome, very pleasant to look at, seems to be a nice enough guy, but he's just not Cash. Plain and simple. My guess is there's only one guy for me. I just hope I'm the only girl for him.

The guy I've been examining raises his eyebrows in question, and I remember what he said.

"Why must I be Olivia?" I ask agreeably. His grin widens. It's contagious and puts me instantly at ease.

"Well, for starters, Olivia is a pretty-girl name. And you're a pretty girl. Secondly, you're the only employee I haven't met here, which means you must be Olivia. Now," he says, leaning in and looking at me from the corner of his eye. "Be honest. You're impressed by my extraordinary powers of deduction, aren't you?"

His eyes are full of mischief and I find myself laughing before I can even reason out what he's saying.

"Okay, you caught me. I won't lie. I'm terribly impressed by your extraordinary powers of deduction."

He nods. "As I suspected. I'm irresistible that way." Abruptly, he straightens and sticks his hand across the bar. "I'm Gavin. Gavin Gibson. I help Cash with the bar."

"Gavin Gibson? That sounds like the real identity of a superhero. You packin' a cape somewhere under that shirt?" I ask.

"Nah, I stow my only superpower in my pants."

He winks and I grin.

"Do you flirt like this with all the employees here, Mr. Gibson?"

"Mr. Gibson?" His expression shows he's clearly appalled. "Mr. Gibson is my father."

"Sorry, *Gavin*."

"Much better. And no, I don't. It's very unprofessional for one thing. But, far more importantly, none of the other employees look like you. If they did, I might have a problem on my hands."

"I never figured you for the sexual-harassment type, Gavin," Cash says, coming to a stop at the bar beside Gavin.

Although his tone is light and playful, Cash's expression is anything but. Gavin leans an elbow on the bar and turns to Cash.

"You've never had an employee worth harassing before," he teases, looking over to wink at me. "But this one might be worth losing my job over."

"Oh, you'd lose more than your job if you ever laid a hand on her. Trust me."

Gavin's still smiling as he looks back at Cash. I see it slowly fade as he takes in Cash's very serious expression. Gavin straightens and his head turns from Cash to me and back again.

He nods and claps Cash on the shoulder with one big hand. They're pretty close to the same size, but Cash is still a touch bigger.

"Got it, mate. No harm intended." He turns to me and gives me another charming smile. "Olivia, it's been a pleasure. If you'll excuse me, we have some business to discuss."

Cash doesn't move until Gavin has already left the bar and is heading in the direction of the office. He looks at me, his eyes deep, fathomless pools of ink, and then he turns and follows Gavin, leaving me baffled as to what just happened.

TEN

Cash

It's all I can do not to slam the office door behind me as I follow Gavin inside. I'm seething. And Gavin knows me well enough to know it.

"I didn't know you were seeing her, bro. I meant no offense."

I know he didn't. But that does nothing to appease my anger. Watching Olivia smile like that for someone else was . . . was . . .

"You can't act like that around employees, Gavin. Do you know the kind of legal shitstorm you could cause?"

He holds up his hands in surrender. "My bad, Cash. It won't happen again. I just wasn't thinking."

"Don't let it happen again. I mean it."

"It won't," he assures me solemnly. After a few seconds of

silence, he makes mistake number two. "But damn, that's one hot sheila!"

His accent seems more pronounced, which only makes me angrier. It's like he's slipped into some mode where he's trying to be more appealing to the women.

"That's enough!" I snap.

Gavin grins and nods slowly, like he's discovered something.

"Ahh, so you *are* seeing her."

"I didn't—"

"You didn't have to. Don't forget that I know you, mate. For a while now. I've seen you with your flavor of the month before and you've never given a shit if I flirt with them or not."

"You've never—"

"The hell I haven't! You've just never noticed before."

I can't even clear my mind enough to think back and determine whether it's true. But I decide it doesn't matter. What matters is that he keeps his hands off Olivia. His eyes, too.

"Olivia's . . . she's . . . it's just . . ."

"Say no more. From now on, she's my little sister."

I look at him. Really look at him. In his eyes, I see my best friend. My business partner. One of the few people on the planet I actually trust. And I know he's telling the truth.

I nod, too. "Good enough."

Gavin sinks down in his chair a little, propping one ankle on his knee and lacing his fingers together behind his head. He's back to his old comfortable self.

"So, what's going on? From what I'm gathering, it must be pretty important."

I'm sure he's referring to my short temper. At least partly. Gavin is a very perceptive guy. His father was military and they moved around a lot. The family was stationed in Australia for several years when Gavin was young, which is where the trace of an accent comes from.

By the time Gavin was a teenager, they were living in Ireland. His father somehow got caught in the middle of two nasty groups of rebels and ended up getting himself, Gavin's mom, and Gavin's older sister killed. It wasn't long after that that Gavin went on to serve in a different kind of military. The kind that doesn't go on résumés and that people sometimes die after finding out about.

He was a mercenary for several years. He's a few years older than me—around thirty, I think—but he's got some of the best tactical skills I've ever seen. He's pretty badass and I'm glad he's my friend and on my side.

Aside from his keen intellect and . . . other experience, he's a pilot. He can fly virtually anything, from Cessnas to small jets to helicopters. In fact, now that he's no longer a merc, that's what he does when he's not helping me with the club—he has a charter business for his chopper.

We met through my father. Dad used Gavin's piloting services a few times when he first started getting things in order to break ties with the *Bratva*, the Russian mafia. Gavin was competent and discreet, and Dad learned quickly that he was a man who could be trusted, especially when it came to doing the right thing, despite the consequences.

Gavin kept in touch with Dad when he went to prison, so

when the economy tanked and Gavin's business started dropping off, Dad put him in touch with me for some extra work. We hit it off instantly. Since that day, Gavin has been my best friend and the closest thing to nonimprisoned family I've had for years.

And now I'm going to need his experience and his discretion more than ever before.

"How much did my dad tell you about what happened to land him in prison?"

Gavin relays what Dad told him and I fill in the blanks. Well, most of them, anyway. I don't tell him about Nash's death, or that I'm living as both brothers and have been for seven years. That's information I'd like to keep to myself as long as possible. That's a level of trust I have in few people. Actually, more like one person.

Olivia.

"So, you have no idea who's gonna be showing up here in the next . . ." Gavin looks at his watch. "Twenty minutes or so?"

"Not a clue. Dad must think or know that they either have some kind of information that can help me or some way of getting us out of this without giving up valuable, one-of-a-kind leverage *or* somebody's life."

"Yeah, making a copy of the books is out of the question. If they ever found out, you know as well as I do, they'd kill you on the spot. If people like that give you *one* chance, they sure as hell won't tolerate any kind of betrayal."

"My concern isn't *only* with giving up the information that could get Dad off. It's as much about how these people work. They don't leave witnesses alive. Ever. I have to figure out some other way to make sure Olivia is safe. Completely. Permanently. I either have to get rid of them or . . . I don't know what. But I have to do something. I have to make sure she's safe."

Gavin rubs his chin. "That could be tricky. These are dangerous people to underestimate. But you're a great strategist. One of the smartest guys I've ever met. And that's saying a lot. I've worked all over the world with all kinds of people. You'd have made an excellent merc. You might not have much to go on now, but once your dad's plan B person gets here, you'll know more. You're a lot like Greg. And, knowing what kind of guy your father is, this mystery person's gonna be a game changer."

I reach up to squeeze the bridge of my nose, hoping to stop the dull throb that's beating just behind my eyes. "I hope you're right. If not, I'm gonna have to come up with something pretty damn fast. I've only got until nine thirty in the morning. They're giving me thirty minutes after the bank opens to get in and get the books. Then I'll be meeting them."

"But the books aren't at the bank, right?"

"No, they're not."

I trust Gavin, but I still hesitate to show my hand.

"Did you tell them which bank?"

"No. Why?'

"Well, that might play into it. Might help you on your time. Plus, they won't be able to meet you there. Try to pull any of their typical tricks."

"Yeah, the longer we have and the less they know, the better."

"Always."

Gavin and I spitball back and forth while we wait. It keeps me from pacing, which is what I feel like doing. I don't like waiting. I don't like not having all the facts. I don't like being the last to know. And, most of all, I don't like worrying about being able to keep Olivia safe. There are too many unknowns, too many players, too many variables. What I need is for Dad's man or people to get here so I can regain some amount of control.

For a while after the accident, I was bloodthirsty. All I could think about was getting revenge against the people who killed my mother and brother, and who framed my father for their deaths. But over time, the more I became Nash the law student, the more I realized there was a legal way to go about it, a way that could free my father. That alone would be worth going about it without bloodshed. So that's what I did. I set about getting my law degree and learning as much as I could about similar cases, so that one day I could use the evidence that my dad had sacrificed so much for to see justice served.

But now all that is in jeopardy. Unless the ace up Dad's sleeve is a damned good one.

Forty-four minutes later, an hour before the club closes, an ace walks through my office door. And holy hell what an ace it is!

ELEVEN

Olivia

It would be impossible not to notice him. Danger and confidence and reckless disregard for pretty much anybody and anything emanate from him like a stink. Or, for every female in the immediate vicinity, like a perfume.

I'm pretty sure that tickle at the back of my throat is Taryn's pheromones. They might choke us all. I don't even have to look down the bar at her to know she's sitting up and taking notice. I wouldn't be surprised if she were preening like a cat. But I could also understand it. He's pretty . . . compelling.

He's tall. Every bit as tall as Cash. The fact that he's wearing a black leather jacket and sunglasses into a club in the middle of the night only makes him stand out that much more. But it's not only that. It's not just one thing. Or ten things. It's *everything* about him. There's no way this guy could hide. Not in the biggest crowd could he go unnoticed.

People step away from him as he walks through the room. I don't know if it's fear or reverence, but something causes them to give him ample space.

I'd guess his hair is chin length. Maybe shoulder length, but pulled back into a ponytail as it is, it's hard to tell. The color is like pale straw, lighter on top than underneath, which makes me think he works out in the sun. Often.

His chin is covered with a thick, light brown goatee. Between that and the sunglasses, most of the details of his face are obscured, but there's something about him that seems vaguely familiar. I wonder if he's been in the club before. Not dressed like this, of course, but maybe in regular clothes.

Without stopping, he walks straight to Cash's office and disappears inside. It's like there's a pause after he's gone, as though his slow, powerful walk across the room left a slight concussion in its wake. But after about thirty seconds, everyone returns to last call as if nothing happened.

But I'm more curious than ever.

TWELVE

Cash

I'm glad I'm sitting when he walks in. I'm also glad I'm not eating or drinking when he walks in. It would be a shame to make it this far and then choke and die from seeing the long-awaited visitor walk into my office.

And recognize that he's my twin brother.

Nash.

"What the fu—"

My first thought, my first *feeling* is profound relief. Joy even. My brother isn't dead. He's very much alive. And standing right in front of me.

His hair is longer. And blonder. His face is familiar. I'd recognize it anywhere, of course. Even with the lower half covered in a dark blond goatee, it looks just like mine. Only harder. Much harder.

I feel the presence of him in a way that no other person on earth feels it. We're part of each other in a way that most siblings don't experience. It's different being a twin.

I think, on some level, I've always known he wasn't dead. I never felt him leave, never felt him die. I never felt his absence like he was truly gone.

But what does this mean? What the hell is going on? It takes me only a few seconds to put the pieces together.

Dad.

"Dad knew. He knew all along and didn't tell me."

A slap in the face. A sucker punch to the balls. A reality check that reminds me there really *isn't* anyone I can trust. Not completely.

I trust Gavin for the most part, but the two people I've trusted the most have both given me reason to question my judgment. My father obviously withheld quite a bit from me. I don't know why, but I'm damn sure going to find out eventually. Once I make sure Olivia is safe . . .

Olivia.

She's the other person I've trusted with a lot. She hasn't betrayed that trust, but she's been withdrawing over the last day or two and it concerns me. I know she has a lot to overcome and deal with, but now isn't the time for that. It's too dangerous for her to decide all of a sudden that I'm not trustworthy and then bolt. It could mean her life.

What that means to me is that either I have to convince Olivia she can trust me, that I'd never hurt her, or I have to

UP TO ME

leave her alone. She can't be safe if she doesn't trust me. And I can't trust *her* if she doesn't trust me.

Nash's words bring me back to his mysterious reappearance. "Yeah. We all had our reasons for making the choices we made. You included," he says pointedly.

He's right, but that doesn't take the sting out of being the only one kept in the dark. My temper rises, but before I lay into Nash, Gavin shifts, reminding me that I'm not alone with my brother.

I glance at my bar manager and best friend, who is looking back and forth between Nash and me. His expression says he's a little confused, but not as much as I might've expected.

"I'll explain all this later," I promise.

Gavin narrows his eyes and then starts to slowly nod. "No, I don't think there's any reason for that. I think I'm up to speed." He gets to his feet and steps over to Nash. "Gavin Gibson. I don't suppose we've met before."

I'll be damned. He did figure it out.

I "met" Gavin as Nash once to add some legitimacy to the farce. If Gavin had ever had any suspicions about the identity, he'd never mentioned it. But then again, knowing Gavin, he'd probably keep it to himself in case he needed it later. I guess in this business—well, my dad's business—everyone has their secrets. And their weapons.

I nod to my friend. No point in holding anything back now.

I turn back to Nash, crossing my arms over my chest. "So, are you gonna bring me up to speed?"

99

Nash watches me. It's in this moment, not when I first saw him and saw how different he looks, that I realize he's changed. He's more like me—the old me, the rebellious me, the bad boy—than he ever was before. Only he's much more dangerous than I ever was.

"I didn't come here to catch up on the last seven years. I came here because Dad sent the message. It must be time to get down to business."

"What's that supposed to mean?'

"I've got leverage."

"So do I. But they know I have it and they're making unacceptable threats, threats I can't risk calling them on."

He stops to watch me again. It's like he's trying to get inside my head. And when he finally speaks again, it seems like he might've been successful.

"Who do they have?"

"A girl I know. Someone they think is important to me."

A slight frown flickers across his forehead, but then it's gone. "Someone they *think* is important to you?" I nod. "But she's not?"

I shrug. "I'm not particularly fond of her. But there is one who *is* important to me. And they know about her, too."

He nods slowly, taking it all in.

"Well, I have enough incriminating evidence to change everything if we use it right."

"Then why haven't you used it before now?"

"Dad. He wanted to wait. He was afraid of putting us in

more danger. That's the only reason he went along with any of this. He's spent the last seven years in prison to protect us, not because he didn't have a way out. He's known all along he holds all the cards. He was just scared of the consequences of using them, of screwing up and killing someone else."

"So the books . . ."

"Were only part of it, yes. But it has kept you safe all this time, so it was worth it. To him."

To him.

I don't know what to make of that last part. Does Nash resent *me*? I don't see how or why he would. He's known the deal all along, while I've been operating under only bits and pieces of information. He's known the truth. I've known mostly lies.

My temper ratchets up another notch. "Man, if you've got something to say, say it. I'm getting real tired of this shit. I don't take kindly to people messing with my life and only telling me half-truths and part of the story. You can either come clean or hit the door. I'll figure out another way. Without you and . . . whatever it is you *think* you've got."

After a few seconds, Nash's lips turn up into a small, cold smile.

"At least you're not a *total* pussy."

I see red. I've had about enough of all this—this life, this deception, this game. I take a step toward Nash, fully intending to plant my fist right in the center of his face. He smirks like he'd welcome it, like he'd welcome the opportunity to trade a few punches with me. But Gavin steps between us.

"If I had to guess, I'd say there are more important things than your pissing contest right now. Focus, mate. Focus. For Olivia, if nothing else."

His eyes are as calm as the shallow blue waters they so closely resemble. Within a few seconds, the wisdom of his words and the person behind them cools my temper.

Olivia.

"This isn't over," I grind out through my gritted teeth. Nash nods once, his smirk still firmly in place. For a fraction of a second, I feel another surge of the desire to beat that smugness out of him, but it's gone almost as soon as it arrived.

"We'll find time later. I look forward to it."

I can see by the hungry look on his face that he does. I don't know what he has to be angry about, but I really don't care, either. I need him for one thing and one thing only. Then he can take his ass back to wherever he came from and we won't ever have to see each other again.

"Well, if you think I'm going in there without knowing what you've got, you couldn't be more wrong. This is going down my way. Period."

Nash's laugh is a short bark. "I don't give a shit about saving your friends. Or your girlfriend. I've been waiting for seven years to take down the people who killed Mom and stole my life. I can wait a few more days. I've got my own agenda."

"I don't care what you do as long as it doesn't interfere with my plans or put anyone I care about in danger."

Nash's lips thin. "You don't care, huh? You don't care that someone blew up our mother? You don't care that someone framed our father? You don't care that he's spent years in prison to protect us? You don't care that somebody took our lives and pissed on 'em, then set 'em on fire?" Nash laughs derisively. "Oh, that's right. You wouldn't. You've been the beneficiary of all our family grief, haven't you, you son of a bitch?"

"What the hell are you talking about? How have I benefited? You mean by pretending to be my perfect brother, by living his perfect life and having to put up with the assholes someone like him would associate with? You mean by spending years grieving the loss of every single member of my family? You mean by visiting my only living relative in a guarded room with glass between us twice a month for seven years, and working day and night to figure out a legal way to get him out? Is that what you mean?"

Nash takes a step toward me. I see Gavin flinch like he's ready to step in again; he didn't move far away to begin with. But Nash stops.

"That sounds a hell of a lot better than spending the last seven years on the run. In hiding. I gave up everything—who I was, what I wanted, all I ever had—to honor my father's wishes. To keep him safe, to keep you safe. I got to sneak into town a few times a year to see my brother living my life. Free.

Happy. Alive. While I had to stay dead. Running guns with smugglers. Stuck on a ship. Every day, for months at a time. I'd trade lives with you any day of the week."

"You can have your life! I never wanted it. Everything I've done, I've done for Dad. Don't think you're the only one who's suffered, Nash."

We stare each other down. We're at an impasse. I'd never admit it, but now I can see why he'd be angry. We've both suffered, both paid for mistakes that weren't ours. But maybe the end is in sight. Maybe it's finally time to be free of the past. Finally.

"I know you boys have a lot to talk about, but it has to wait. We've only got a few hours to get a plan together. What do you say we put the bullshit aside and get down to business?"

I look to Gavin. His expression hasn't changed from the pleasant one that he always wears. Sometimes it's hard to believe he's deadly. But he is. He just hides it well. That probably makes him even more dangerous.

"You're right. We don't have time for this." I glance at the clock on the wall. "It'll be time to close soon. I'll have to bring Olivia back and fill her in on some of what's going on."

"Do you think that's really the smart thing to do?" Nash snaps.

"Yes, as a matter of fact I do. She needs to know. She has a *right* to know. Her life is in danger because of me. Because of *us*. Hell yeah, I think it's the smart thing. The more cooperative she is, the better."

Nash rolls his eyes and shakes his head. Obviously he dis-agrees. But, again, I couldn't care less. He doesn't have to agree with me; he just has to give me what I need to make sure Olivia's safe. Permanently. Then I don't give a rat's ass what he does.

THIRTEEN

Olivia

Strange huge men keep disappearing into Cash's office, so when the bar closes, I'm a little nervous about going back there. But I go. I don't really have much of a choice. I'm in way over my head.

As I reach beneath the bar and grab my purse, I hear the door to the office open. A sliver of light pours out onto the floor and I hear voices. Low, deep voices. My stomach curls into a tight knot.

The door opens farther and Cash's big body blocks most of the light. His eyes lock onto mine immediately. "Are you done?"

I nod.

He turns back and speaks to someone behind him, then emerges to walk across the room and lock the front doors. I watch him, afraid to move. Without my work and all the customers in the bar, the tension is sliceable.

How did I get myself into this mess?

Before I can formulate some kind of answer, Cash is walking toward me, his face hard and intense. "Let's go back to my office. There are some things I need to tell you."

My pulse picks up and dread runs through my veins like ice water. Cash meets me at the cutout at the end of the bar. When I step out in front of him, he puts his hand at the small of my back and guides me to his office. I can feel the warmth of his palm through my shirt, and it comforts me.

I ease through the door to find Gavin in Cash's chair behind the desk and the tall stranger with the ponytail across from him, his back to me. Gavin looks up and smiles.

"There she is."

I smile in return, although I'm sure it's tight. My face feels like it might crack from the tension. In just a few short hours, Cash will be going to get Marissa. Who knows what will happen then?

Acid sloshes in my belly and saliva pours into my mouth. I close my eyes and take a slow, deep breath.

When I open them, the stranger is rising to his feet. He turns toward me, leaning back against the desk and crossing his arms over his wide chest. He's taken his glasses off. And it makes all the difference in the world.

My heart skips a beat as I look into the familiar blackbrown of Cash's eyes. Only they're not Cash's. Not exactly.

Cash steps around in front of me to stand beside the

stranger. As I look from one to the other, I don't need to ask who the stranger is, but I do need someone to explain to me how he's here, how he's standing in front of me when he's supposed to be dead.

Sweet hell! This is even worse than I thought!

"Nash," I say quietly, trying to sound calm when I feel anything but.

He smiles, a gesture that doesn't quite reach his eyes. "Very good." He looks to Cash. "At least this one has a brain."

I don't know what that's supposed to mean, but I can't worry about it right now. I just want to find out what's going on, what's expected of me, and how we can all get safely out of this crazy and surprisingly dangerous dilemma. Everything else will just have to wait.

"You look pretty good for a dead guy."

"My brother's done a great job of keeping me alive, don't you think?"

There's no mistaking the bitterness in his tone.

"I suppose so. You don't seem too happy about that."

"Why would I be happy that someone is pretending to be me?"

Temper flashes in his eyes. It gives me pause, but only a little bit. For some reason, with Cash close, I'm not afraid of him. I might be otherwise, but right now, I feel brave.

"Why would you *not* be? You got off easy. You have a law degree that you didn't have to study for, a job you didn't have to work for, and a life you didn't have to earn. Sounds like Cash has done the hard part."

I glance at Cash. He's watching me. He smiles. It's wide and pleased. Smug almost. He winks one twinkling eye at me, and I feel the heat rush to my face. He must be happy that I'm standing up for him.

Nash straightens and takes one step forward. My first inclination is to back up, even though he's not that close to me. But I don't. I hold my ground. "That might be true, especially if you don't have a damn clue about what my life was like. Like if you didn't know that I had to give up my entire identity and go to work for criminals on a smuggling boat. Or if you didn't know that I could only come to shore once every few months. Or if you didn't know that I had to sneak into town wearing a disguise, only to see my brother living a great life. *My* life. Yeah, I can see where you'd think I'd be grateful."

Guilt washes through me. I don't know what to say. I look to Cash, who is watching Nash, his face set in hard lines. I glance at Gavin, who seems bored with the whole conversation. Then I glance back to Nash, who suddenly looks broken and bereaved behind his stony mask.

"I'm so sorry," I confess sincerely. "I-I didn't know. I just assumed . . ."

Nash's laugh is a short snap. "Yeah, well you know what they say about assuming."

He steps back to resume his position against the desk. I don't take any offense at his words. He has every right to them. Both he and Cash have gotten the shaft and I feel incredibly sorry for both of them, for what they've suffered and what they've lost, for what they've had to go through for a man who made all the wrong decisions.

"Maybe after this, you won't have to hide anymore," I say softly.

Nash stares into my eyes. I can see that he wants to believe that's true, and my heart squeezes painfully. "Maybe. Maybe one day I can have the freedom, the job, the life. The girl."

I don't know if he means me per se, but his look is so intense, it makes me blush, anyway.

Holy wow! He's so much like his brother.

Cash moves to stand at my side. When he speaks, his voice is strained. "If we do this right, maybe we can both have our lives back. And you can find your own job and life and girl."

Cash slides an arm around my waist. I want to smile at the possessive gesture. Men and their silly posturing!

Obviously, the conversation needs a new direction. The tension is killing me!

"So, have you figured out what to do about tomorrow?"

I hear Cash sigh.

Uh-oh.

"I think so."

He moves away from me to pace to the apartment door and back, his head bent in thought.

"Well?"

"Nash has some . . . information that we can use as leverage after handing over the books for Marissa."

"What kind of information?"

There's a pause, during which it feels like everyone in the room is debating the wisdom of answering me. I disabuse them of that notion right away. "If you're thinking of keeping me in the dark when I'm one of the ones in their crosshairs, you really need to think again. You need my cooperation, right? I mean, I could go right to the cops and that would change everything, right?"

I hate to make such a threat. I think Cash knows I'm just bluffing, but the others don't. There's no way they could.

It's Gavin who speaks up first. "Just tell her, mate. You're the one who says she can be trusted."

I won't lie. It makes me very happy that Cash has told them as much. It also makes me feel guilty for the misgivings I've had the last couple of days.

"The afternoon of the accident, Nash was coming back from the store with supplies for the trip. He stopped on the dock of the marina to video a couple of girls lying on top of a yacht, sunbathing topless. He accidentally caught the trigger-man on tape."

"Triggerman?"

"Yeah, the guy who detonated the bomb."

I gasp. "Oh, shit!"

"Exactly. They'd have killed all of us if they'd known Nash had it. I think Dad was right to hold off for a while. Something like that is very dangerous."

"So you're going to hand over the books and then what? Use the video to . . ."

"Keep us all alive."

"But how? It'll be just like the books all over again, only they'll know who has it, who to go after."

I feel sick. I can only imagine the kinds of torture they'd employ upon loved ones to get their hands on evidence as damning as a video.

"Not exactly. There's something else at play. Dad had me send two messages. Nash was one. We haven't heard from the other one yet. Nash thinks that the video used in conjunction with this other . . . player might be enough to get us out of this forever."

"Forever? How exactly?"

"By eliminating the threat."

"What's that supposed to mean? That sounds like you plan to kill somebody."

"No. Not us."

I look between the faces of the three guys. They're all very serious.

"Surely you're joking."

Not one of them even flinches.

"You can't really be considering this."

Still nothing.

My head spins. It's just like the movies. But it's so much worse in real life. For a few seconds, it seems surreal. I can't wrap my mind around being involved in something like this. I mean, this is . . . this is . . .

Cash moves in front of me and bends until his face is inches from mine. "Olivia, these are bad men. And I don't mean they've robbed a liquor store. These men are killers. Murderers.

And they won't stop if they think for one second that any of us poses a threat. Or could get them something they want. This is real. And it's serious."

I search his eyes. I guess, considering the conversation, I'm looking for a monster. But I don't find one. I see only the guy I've been falling more and more in love with. I wonder if it's too late to turn back now.

"What are you asking of me?"

His eyes never leaving mine, Cash straightens. "Give us a minute, guys," he says to Gavin and Nash. Quietly, they make their way from the room. Cash takes my hand and leads me through the door at the back of the office, into the kitchen of the apartment area in behind. When he releases my hand, I lean against the cabinets to keep from falling over. My heart is pounding so loudly I wonder if Cash can hear it.

Cash's back is to me. I see him run his fingers through his hair and I hear him sigh again. "I'm asking you to trust me, Olivia." He turns to face me. "Trust in what you *know* about me. Because I know, if you stop listening to your fear, you know who I am. Deep down. You know me, Olivia. You *know me*."

His voice is sincere. His expression is urgent. I close my eyes against his face, his handsome face, the face that haunts both my waking and my sleeping world. I open them again when I feel warm hands cup my cheeks. Cash is a breath away, his eyes oceans of midnight, drawing me out into the deep.

"It's me," he says softly. "Stop listening to everything else. Remember the way you feel when I'm kissing you and touching you. Don't think with your head. You know me. And when my lips are on yours, you trust me." As if to make his point, he dips his head and brushes his mouth over mine. Sparks fly between us. As always. "You trust me, when my hands are on your skin." He runs his palms down my arms and then over to my waist, where he pushes them up under the edge of my shirt. Chills break out down my back. "You trust me when you turn your mind off, when you just feel."

His hands move farther up, skating over my ribs to cup my breasts. His thumbs brush my nipples, and then he squeezes them through the thin material of my bra. I catch my breath.

"See? You aren't thinking. You're just feeling. You're feeling me. Right now you trust me. You know I'd do anything for you, that I'd never hurt you. You know you're not like the others. I know you know that. And that you want me. Just like I want you."

He's right. He's right about all of it. And I do want him. I always have. In a way it makes no sense that I'd want him right now considering what might be happening in the next few hours. But in a way, it makes perfect sense. If things go wrong, this might be the last time I see Cash, or get to be with him this way.

That thought brings with it both panic and abandon. I swallow the words that want to rush out, words about love and devotion, words that have no place in this moment. They deserve to be spoken when there's no pressure and no distress. And that's not now.

But we still have tonight. So I'll show him. I'll give him everything else I have.

"Tell me you want me," he commands softly, his voice a low growl.

I don't hesitate. Reaching up, I drag my fingertip along his perfect lower lip. "I want you."

"Tell me you trust me."

"I trust you."

He exhales, his warm breath fanning my face. "Now tell me you want me to touch you."

His hands are still, unmoving over my bra. But I don't want them to be still. More than anything, I want them to move. "I want you to touch me."

His eyes are pure heat, searing mine. He watches me as he pulls the cups of my bra down. His palms are rough as they glide over my nipples, making them pucker. He pinches them between his fingers, and lava pours into my core. I bite back a moan.

"Tell me you want me to lick your nipples, to suck them into my mouth." His voice is like black velvet. It slides over my skin like a tangible thing.

"I want you to lick my nipples." I'm already breathless as he pulls my tank over my head. His eyes are back on mine as he reaches behind me to unhook my bra.

"Finish," he demands, refusing to give me what I want until I spell it out.

"I want you to suck them into your mouth."

Bending his head, Cash flicks one nipple with his tongue, then draws it into his hot mouth. I thread my fingers through his hair, holding him to me.

He sucks on one, biting it lightly, before he moves to the other to give it the same treatment. When he lifts his head, there's fire in his eyes.

"Tell me to unzip your pants."

Even though I can barely speak, I don't hesitate. "Unzip my pants."

In one quick movement, he flips open the button and unzips my pants.

"Tell me you want me to put my fingers inside you."

His voice is hoarse and his hand is resting just a few inches away from where I want it most. The anticipation of feeling him is almost too much to bear.

"I want you to put your fingers inside me."

Turning his palm toward my body, he slides his hand into my panties and pushes two long fingers inside me. My knees go weak and I reach behind me to hold on to the countertop for support.

Cash closes his eyes and moans a little. "Oh my God, you're so wet. Do you know what that does to me?"

I nod. "Yes." I know because I feel it, too.

"Tell me you want me to taste you."

Slowly, he drags his finger in and out of me. My hips move with him.

"Taste me."

Pulling his hand free from me, he raises one glistening finger and slips it into his mouth. I'm mesmerized.

"That's the best taste in the world," he says. "Tell me you want a taste, too. I want to watch you lick my finger."

More heat rushes between my legs. "I want a taste, too," I breathe obediently.

Cash bends and, with one quick jerk, pulls my pants down to my ankles. As he rises, he pauses to press his lips to the outside of my panties, kissing me. I want to beg him to stop there, but before I can speak, he's taking my breath away with his wicked fingers.

Pushing my panties to the side, Cash thrusts two fingers inside me, burying them deep and bringing me up onto my toes. He crooks them within me as he massages my clitoris with his thumb. He looks up and his eyes find mine again.

Slowly, he straightens and brings one finger to my lips. His eyes drop to my mouth as I open it. He drags his wet fingertip over my bottom lip, then looks back up at me. "Lick." I lick my bottom lip, tasting the salty sweetness there. "So good," he whispers before he slides his finger into my mouth, rubbing it over my tongue. I close my lips around it and suck until I hear the air hiss through his gritted teeth.

"Tell me you want me inside you."

"I want you. Inside me. Right now," I pant desperately.

I can't take my eyes off his. Even as I hear the sound of his zipper, our gaze is locked together. I reach down to push my panties over my hips just before Cash grabs me under the arms and puts me up on the counter. The granite is cool against my butt, making me long for the heat of his body.

Still watching me, always watching me, Cash pulls one shoe off my foot, then eases my pants and panties down over it, freeing one leg.

"Spread your legs for me."

I do as he asks.

His eyes on my moist, sensitive flesh make me feel even hotter, even wetter. Cash wraps his fingers around his shaft, stroking it slowly from base to tip, making my muscles clench in anticipation of him filling me. "Now tell me what you want."

"I want you inside me."

"What do you want me to do there?"

"I want you to come in me, to come *with* me."

I hear his moan just before he lets his desire off the leash. It seems that one moment he's inches away; the next he's touching me. All over, everywhere at once.

His hands are in my hair, at my breasts, on my back. His lips are on mine, at my ear, on my neck. His tongue is teasing mine, teasing my nipples, teasing my navel.

Then his hands are sliding under my hips. The world tilts when he picks me up off the counter. Just as my legs wrap around his waist, he enters me, pulling me down onto him, seating himself so far inside me that it steals my breath.

As my head falls back on my shoulders, I cry out. I can't help it. I'm lost to everything but Cash. I barely hear my own voice. It's like a soft echo of what's going on between us—a tornado of sensation and heavy breathing, a hurricane of lips and tongues and teeth and fingers.

I hear Cash's breath in my ear. I feel his body inside mine. I feel the air rushing over my skin as he carries me to the bed.

Then there's a firm mattress at my back and a warm body

on top of mine. He's moving inside me, hard and powerful, each thrust deeper than the last.

The buildup is too much, the pleasure too strong. My body feels like it's coming apart at the seams. Just before I squeeze my eyes shut, I see Cash come up onto his knees. I give myself up to feeling as he spreads my legs wide and rubs my most sensitive part with his thumb, all the while driving in and out of me.

And then I'm toppling over the edge. The first wave of my orgasm makes me dizzy. I hear Cash saying my name over and over. I open my eyes to see him arch his back and pound into me with a recklessness that bursts in my body like a shower of fireworks.

The walls absorb his groan as his pace slows to longer, more languid strokes. His body still pulses within me. Then, with one final thrust, he collapses onto me.

We rest together, drifting back down to earth. His breathing is heavy in my ear. When it becomes less labored, I feel the first press of his lips against my neck. It's one of a thousand tiny kisses he rains over my throat and my face. When he lifts his head, his eyes meet mine. I'm not sure what they say, but I think my heart understands.

FOURTEEN

Cash

With Olivia tucked along my side, I really don't want to move. But I have to. Reality—and danger—are lurking just around the corner, on the other side of daylight, which is just a few short hours away.

Olivia is tracing the tattoo on the left side of my chest, like she often does when we lie naked together. I don't know if it's soothing to her, but it is to me.

Her fingers start to move more and more slowly until they stop. Her breathing becomes deep and even. She's so still I know she's asleep. I'm sure she's exhausted. But there's nothing I can do about that yet.

I slide out from under her as gently as I can, but I still wake her.

"Rest, baby. I'll be right back."

I can see that her eyes are open and focused on mine, so I know she heard me. She doesn't answer, though. She just smiles.

After straightening my clothes, I head out through the office to the club. Nash and Gavin are sitting at the bar, pouring shots from a bottle of whiskey.

"Help yourself," I remark smartly as I approach.

"Oh, don't worry. We have," Gavin replies with a cheeky grin.

I pull up a stool and a shot, downing it in one quick swallow. The burn is welcome. It reminds me that there will be much pain and loss if I don't do this just right. The first time. There's no doubt that I won't get a second chance.

"I was thinking about it, and I feel like the only place Olivia will really be safe is with her mother."

"That's what you were doing back there? Thinking about that chick's *mother*?" Nash asks snidely. "If she mentions needing a real man, send her my way."

"Spending so much time alone with a bunch of men on a boat, I'm sure you could recommend one."

Gavin spits whiskey across the bar.

Nash stands so quickly his stool falls over. "What the hell is that supposed to mean?"

I stand, too. "It means that you even *think* about touching her, talking to her, so much as *looking* at her, and we're gonna have a big, big problem, *bro*."

Before Nash and I can get chest to chest, Gavin steps between us. Again.

"I'm not going to be able to leave you two alone at all, am I?"

He gives us each a little shove, which, coming from Gavin, is nearly enough to send us back a step. Nearly, but not quite.

Gavin pours three more shots and slides one to me and one to Nash, picking up the third and holding it up between us. "To safety and success. Salut!"

Nash and I are still eyeing each other, but we toast to Gavin. It's a good sentiment, one worth taking a moment to recognize.

After a short pause, I clear my throat, saying pointedly, "As I was saying, I was thinking that the only place Olivia can really be safe is at her mother's. Since her parents divorced, Olivia hasn't been close to her. They rarely talk, and I doubt anyone would be able to find her there very easily. In fact, I'm not even sure where she lives. Seems like I heard Olivia mention Savannah, but I can't be sure. At any rate, I'll find out."

"So you're sending her there, hoping they won't follow you? And that you'll make it back in time?" Nash asks sharply. I grit my teeth and try not to take exception to his tone.

"No, I'm sending her with Gavin. You and I are going to be taking care of the trade tomorrow."

Nash smirks. "Afraid to leave her alone with me, huh?"

"Yes. I am. She needs protection. Competent protection. That's why I'm sending Gavin. I *know* he's capable of keeping her safe."

Nash rolls his eyes but says nothing. At least he's learning to keep his mouth shut.

I turn to Gavin. "Man, I'm trusting you."

He looks me in the eye, and I try to convey all that I mean when I say that. I'm trusting him to respect me by not touching her. I'm trusting him to keep my secrets, to keep Olivia safe, to do whatever he has to in order to protect her. This is not a simple request, and he knows it. The fact that he pauses to really consider what I'm asking makes me feel somewhat better, like he's not taking it lightly.

"I know, mate. You know I've got your back. And hers. We're brothers." Gavin holds out his hand, arm bent at the elbow. When I take it, we're both agreeing to do right by one another, no matter what the cost. This isn't a game. We both know that.

"Brothers," I repeat.

"I hope he's a better brother to you than he was to me," Nash mumbles from the other side of Gavin as he pours himself another drink.

I ignore him.

"I'll find out exactly where you're taking her, where her mom is living now. Give me a few minutes' head start and then meet me at the hotel. Sound good?"

Gavin nods. "Sounds good. And safe. Just make sure you're not followed." I give Gavin a look, and he grins and throws up his hands. "Sorry. Habit. I know you're as careful as you can be."

"Especially when it's important."

He nods again. "And this girl is obviously very important."

I don't answer. I don't know what to say. It's true, of course. I just haven't really thought of it that way—of her being important to me or the exact *degree* to which she's important to me.

But it's a lot. There's no doubt about that.

"Just stick with the plan and do what I ask and I think we

can pull this off." I look behind Gavin to Nash. He's pretending to ignore me. "Can I trust you to do what needs to be done?"

Slowly, Nash turns his cool eyes on me. "Yes, but when it's over, and you and your girlfriend are all safe and sound, it's my turn. My turn to get what I want."

Revenge is in his eyes. I recognize it because I fought the urge for a lot of years. And I lost, for the most part. I just found less . . . violent ways to exact it. Or at least to try. Giving up these books will set me back years—all my plans to use the legal system to incriminate the Russian mafia and to free my father— but it's worth it to make sure Olivia's safe. I can start again, maybe talk some sense into Nash and get him to let me use what he's got. I don't know, but I can't worry about all that now. Tonight the most important thing is getting Olivia to safety. Tomorrow will come soon enough.

"Fair enough. But right now, it's my way."

He looks at me long and hard before he nods.

FIFTEEN

Olivia

Rest? While he's out there plotting and planning with his not-dead twin brother and probably-more-than-he-seems club manager? I think not!

By the time Cash comes back in, I'm up and dressed. Waiting.

As always, just the sight of him kindles a fire in the pit of my stomach. His very presence touches me. It's undeniable.

I take a deep breath, pushing those feelings aside so I can think.

"So, what's the plan?"

Cash looks back out into his office. "Have a seat. We'll be right back out." I hear snickering that presumably belongs to the pleasant and mildly flirtatious Gavin. I can't imagine Nash snickering. I can barely imagine him smiling. I think his default mode is "menace."

Cash closes the door and turns to me. I can see by his expression that he thinks I'm not going to like what he's about to say, which makes me think I won't.

I sigh. "This must be a humdinger."

He chuckles. "What? I haven't even said anything yet."

"You don't have to. That look says it all. It makes my butt pucker."

"Makes your butt pucker?" I nod, and he laughs outright. Shaking his head, an amused expression still on his face, Cash reaches out and pulls me into his arms, snugging me up against his chest. "You're crazy, you know that, right?"

"Of course. Was it supposed to be a secret?"

"No, I think that ship has sailed."

I turn my head slightly and bite his flat male nipple.

"Ouch! Keep doing that and you'll get the best damn spanking you've ever had."

"I've never been spanked before, so the bar is set very low."

"Well, that'll be the first thing on the agenda when I get you back home, then."

I lean farther back. "Get me back home? Where am I going?"

Cash sighs. "Your mother's house. It's the safest place for you right now."

I push out of his arms. "What? You can't be serious! There are a dozen places I can think of right off the top of my head that would be safe *and* give me a reasonable expectation of retaining my sanity. Why in the world would you want me there?"

"Because there is a recent trail to almost everyone else in your life. Everyone except her. You haven't talked to her in how long?"

"A couple years, but that's not the point."

"That's exactly the point. Where else would you be less expected to go?"

My mind goes completely blank, probably because he's right.

Dammit!

"Fine, but you'll have to let me drive myself. She would never understand something like this."

Already, Cash is shaking his head. "Nope. Sorry. Gavin will be taking you and staying with you until it's time to bring you back."

"What? No way! If I have to take someone, why can't it be you?" The more I think of it, the more I like that scenario. That way, Cash would be sure to be safe.

"Gavin is the most . . . capable one of us. You'll be safe with him, no matter what comes up."

"Are you expecting an army of mafia bandits to accost me at my mother's house?"

"I'm not expecting anything. But I'm going to be prepared for . . . whatever."

"If Gavin's the most capable one, maybe you should send him to make the trade with Nash."

"I have to go. I have to do this. I can't trust Nash with it. I need to make sure it gets done and it gets done right. I can't have them threatening you, Olivia. This has to stop."

"But . . . but . . ."

I can't think of a single argument other than I want him with me and I want him to be safe. Neither of those is enough to change his mind, though.

"This is the best way. The *only* way. Just trust me. Can you do that?"

Cash's head is tilted slightly to the side and he's looking deep into my eyes. He's so sincere.

I feel the sting of tears at the backs of my eyes. With a fist lodged in my throat, I don't even try to speak. I just nod and drop my eyes to Cash's mouth.

Tenderly, he pulls me back into his arms. He strokes my hair and rubs circles on my back. "I'll keep you safe. I promise."

"It's not me I'm worried about," I murmur against his chest.

SIXTEEN

Cash

The ride to the hotel with Olivia is a special kind of torture. Even after devouring her an hour ago, I still feel that familiar twitch in my dick when her hands stray too low on my stomach. With my eyes wide open, I can still picture her tiny hands wrapped around my shaft, picture her lips closing over the glistening tip.

And thoughts like that aren't helping.

The other thing that makes it torture is knowing that I'm leaving her in someone else's hands. I hate that. I told her Gavin is the most capable, which is probably true from a technical standpoint. But I feel like there is no one who would risk more for her, no one else who would care as much for her safety as I would. As I *do*.

But it has to be done. My presence alone brings danger right

131

to her doorstep. And that's unacceptable. Until I get this situation under control, this is the best thing for her.

Even if it doesn't feel like the best thing for me.

Olivia is quiet all the way through the lobby, in the elevator, and into the room. She doesn't say a word as she packs what few things she'd taken out of her bag back into it. I feel the need to lighten things up for her. I don't want her leaving on this note. I don't want *either one of us* leaving on this note.

Before she zips her bag, I pull out a pair of her panties and hold them up.

"Can I keep these? I promise they won't end up strung up in the bar."

"Give me those," she says halfheartedly, reaching for them.

I jerk them away from her grasping fingers.

"No. I think I've earned at least one pair."

"So you like girls' underwear, huh? I never would've guessed it."

"They don't make 'em big enough for what I'd have to put in them," I tease.

She grins at that and replies, "Fine. Keep them. I think I've got plenty to last me for a while."

I peek inside her bag. "Oh, yeah. You're good. I mean, you won't be changing them nearly as often without me around." I give her my most devilish grin and feel gratified when her cheeks turn rosy.

"That's probably true. In fact, now that I think about your

effect on my underwear, *you* probably owe *me* several pairs. I seem to remember a couple getting torn."

"Mmm, that's right. How could I forget? I'm surprised your dad didn't hear all that moaning you were doing."

Her mouth drops open and her cheeks burn a little brighter. "Maybe that was *you*. I seem to remember you being extremely excited."

"Baby, I was *very* excited. You do all kinds of delicious things to me. Which makes me want to do all kinds of delicious things to you."

"Um, I'm pretty sure you did."

"Listen, why don't you just 'accidentally' leave all these at your mother's house? If you come home without any, I promise I'll make sure you don't miss them for one second."

"Commando's not my thing. Now Ginger, on the other hand . . ."

"Oh, God!" I exclaim, closing my eyes and turning my head.

"What? Ginger's gorgeous!"

"If you're into that sort of thing."

"What's 'that sort of thing'?"

"Well, she's just so . . . blond and so . . . plastic and so . . . feline."

Olivia laughs. "I thought guys liked that kind of thing."

"Some do."

"Well, evidently you do, too. Taryn is all those things, too, only Ginger has a personality."

"Okay, then I *used to* like that kind of thing. *Now* I like *your* kind of thing. It's the very best kind of thing. Makes all other kinds of things look like shit."

"Well, far be it for me to cause you to conjure mental images of shit without panties."

"Can we not talk about shit and panties in the same sentence?"

"You're the one who was talking about panties and lack thereof."

"Oh my God! I can barely remember that far back. Too many traumatic things have been said since then."

"It was forty-five seconds ago."

"Told you it was traumatic."

She laughs again, and this time, the sparkle in her eye is back. Just like I like it.

SEVENTEEN

Olivia

Cash's teasing makes it easy to forget what's about to happen, but the sharp knock at the door brings reality with it.

"Who's that?" I ask.

"Gavin."

"We're leaving from here?"

"Yes. I thought it would be safer. On the off chance anyone followed me here, they wouldn't see Gavin and know to look for him. He should be parked on the next street over. This way I know no one will see you and be able to follow you to your mom's. They'll still be watching for me."

"So you'll be by yourself." Fear nips at my insides, making them quiver.

"Just for a while. Nash and I have a plan for tomorrow."

"Care to tell me what that is? Or would you rather I not know?"

He eyes me with a strange expression. I'm not sure what to make of it. My mind and my heart are all over the place.

"I don't mind you knowing if you're interested."

"Of course I'm interested! I'm worried about you!"

"Hey, I'm just asking. I don't want to assume anything with you."

That sparks my anger. How in the world could he think I'm not interested? Granted, I've had some doubts resurface over the last day or two, but I don't think I've ever given him the impression that I don't care.

Have I?

The momentary uncertainty is like a wake-up call. I can't let all this go down with Cash thinking that I don't care. I couldn't live with that.

"Cash, I'm very interested. And I care very much about what happens to you. I know I've got some . . . issues to work out, but that has more to do with me than you. You're . . . you're . . ." Words fail me as my throat closes around a knot of agony. I pause to regroup before I continue. "You're important to me. And I know you're a good guy. Deep down, I know it. And I trust you. I really do. It's just hard to describe how I feel sometimes. But please, please don't ever think I don't care."

He smiles down at me, moving in to brush his lips over mine. "Okay, okay. I believe you. And I know what you're saying. I feel the same way." His expression sobers. "It's not always easy for me to say what I feel, but I want you to know I—"

"You two all right in there?" Gavin calls from the hall, pounding on the door again and interrupting Cash.

"Just a minute," Cash snaps gruffly. When he turns back to me, he sighs. He doesn't continue. The moment is lost.

My heart sinks. I would give anything to hear where that sentence was going.

"We can discuss all this when you get back. I can tell you about how our plan went off without a hitch and how I ended the day kicking my arrogant brother's ass, and you can tell me how you explained Gavin to your mother and how she passed out on the floor."

He grins.

"Oh, shit!"

"What?"

"What *am* I gonna tell her?"

Cash shrugs. "You'll have to think of something, because Gavin won't be leaving that house. And you won't be leaving his sight."

"I guess I could tell her we're seeing each other." As I chew my lip in thought, I see the muscle in Cash's jaw tick. I frown. "What?"

"Nothing."

"No, not nothing. What?"

"You're creative. I'm sure you can think of something else to tell her."

"What difference does it make?"

"If she thinks you two are together, she'll expect to see some affection."

"So?"

"So, I'd hate to have to kick Gavin's ass. And then kick yours."

I can tell the last was added teasingly. I can't help but grin.

"Kick it? I thought you wanted to spank it." I'm not normally so brazen, but under the circumstances, I feel like the gloves should come off.

I see desire flare to life in his sinfully dark eyes. It kindles heat low in my belly.

"Whatever I do to it, I promise I'll kiss it and make it feel better afterward. How's that?"

His fingers are trailing lazily up and down my arms. It's an innocent touch but more than enough to make me wish his hands were on my naked skin elsewhere.

"Promises, promises," I purr in challenge.

"I guess I'll just have to show you when you get back, then. And if you happen to be wearing panties, make it a pair you hate. It'll be the last time you see them intact. Consider yourself warned."

A thrill of anticipation skitters down my spine. When Cash loses control, it always ends in us lying, exhausted, in a sweaty heap somewhere. And I wouldn't have it any other way.

"Duly noted."

Gavin pounds once more on the door. Cash winks at me before he turns and crosses the room to pull it open.

"Damn, you're aggravating."

Gavin's smile is full of mischief. "Here I was hoping to get a glimpse of something good, but you let her get dressed." The punch Cash gives his arm seems a little less than gentle. Still grinning, Gavin looks to me. "You ready?"

I heft my bag up over my shoulder. "I guess."

I cross to stop in front of Cash. "Gavin can fill you in on the details since we were *so rudely interrupted*," he says meaningfully, glaring at his buddy.

"Just be careful. Promise me you won't take any unnecessary risks."

"I promise."

Rather than the tiny peck I figured he'd give me in front of his friend, Cash pulls me into his arms and kisses me. Really kisses me. My toes are curled and I'm breathless when he lets me go.

"Don't forget," he says quietly, his eyes roaming my face like he's memorizing it.

"I won't."

I don't know what he's referring to—don't forget what he told me, don't forget his promises? Don't forget him? It doesn't matter, though. It still has a ring of finality to it that makes me feel like this is the end.

I can't stop my chin from trembling as Gavin leads me from the room.

Gavin is quiet as he smuggles me down the stairs—all the zillion stairs—and out a side door. The night air is cooler than average. It's like a slap in the face when I feel it hit the wet streaks on my cheeks. I didn't even know I'd been crying.

Maybe that's why Gavin is so quiet. He thinks I'm about to melt down.

Which I might be. Sometimes I feel like it.

As we strike out up the street, Gavin reaches over to take my bag strap off my shoulder. I offer him a small smile and let him have it.

"He'll be fine, you know," Gavin says quietly, his accent seemingly more pronounced in the dark.

"You can't know that."

"Actually, I can. He's a sharp guy and he's got a good plan. But even more than that, he'd go through hell and back to make sure you're safe. And when he gets a bug up his ass like this, he's like a pit bull. There's just no stopping him."

His words are bittersweet. It thrills me to hear that he thinks I'm that important to Cash. Cash must've said or done something to make him think that. Unless, of course, he'd be asshole enough to lie just to make me feel better. Even so, it just makes me feel sad and bereft that there's a chance I might not ever get to tell Cash I'm in love with him.

Why the hell didn't you tell him five minutes ago? When you had the chance? Oh, wait. I know. Because you're a complete, proud idiot, that's why.

My chest gets tight just thinking about my lost opportunity. I slow to a stop on the street; the urge to go back and throw myself into Cash's arms is nearly overwhelming.

"Gavin, I need to go back. There's something I have to tell him before he goes."

Urgency is coursing through my veins like heroin.

Ohmigod, ohmigod, ohmigod, what have I done?

Panic, sheer panic is working a fine sheen of sweat onto my brow, despite the chilly temperature.

"It's too late," Gavin says gravely. I look into his handsome, sober face, and, just as I open my mouth to argue, a motorcycle zooms by. "He's already gone."

I feel the tears start afresh. "But there's something I need to tell him, something I need him to know before he goes."

Gavin puts his hand on my shoulder and leans down to look into my eyes. "He knows."

"No, he doesn't. He couldn't possibly. I've been such a psycho lately, there's no way he could know."

Gavin grins. "Most women are, but that's beside the point. Trust me, he knows. There's no way he'd be doing all this for a girl who didn't love him."

If Gavin knows, maybe Cash does, too. Maybe he was going to confess his love to me before Gavin interrupted. Oh, if only we'd had a few more minutes . . .

For a second, I want to punch Gavin right in his pretty mouth.

"Damn you!" I rail at him, stomping my foot. "This is your fault! If you hadn't come and knocked when you did—"

Gavin laughs. Laughs! The nerve! "I'm so sorry if my efforts to help save your life are untimely."

I feel my lips tighten and my temper boil. His levity isn't helping matters.

"Don't change the subject. It's not helping," I say through gritted teeth.

Still smiling, Gavin starts walking away, up the street. "Fine. Blame me that you were too afraid to tell him how you feel. But you and I both know it's not my fault."

So smug. So exasperatingly, aggravatingly smug.

And so right.

It's no one's fault but my own.

I stand, rigid and angry, watching Gavin walk away. The farther he walks, the more my irrational irritation drains away. I scurry up the sidewalk to catch him.

"Stop walking so fast, you crazy foreigner!" I mutter.

In front of me, Gavin tips his head back and loudly whispers up into the night, "Walk faster, psycho sheila."

I can't help but smile at that.

Gavin drives an HT3, the Hummer with a tiny truck bed at the back. It's solid black with deeply tinted windows.

"Good God, did you steal this from a drug dealer?"

"Watch it. This baby might well save your sweet ass before it's over. She's about as tactically equipped as they come."

"So you *did* steal it from a drug dealer?"

Gavin rolls his eyes and shakes his head. "Women," he murmurs.

"I hope you don't say things like that in front of your girl-friend."

"Girlfriend?" By the look on his face, you'd think I suggested he was having sex with animals. "That's trouble I don't need. All that emotional shit just messes up great sex and someone to have a few laughs with."

Of course, I draw a parallel. "Is that the way Cash thinks, too?"

Gavin glances over at me. There's caution written in his eyes. "Maybe a little."

"You wouldn't tell me the truth even if that were the case, would you?"

"Look, Olivia. I'll admit Cash and I are pretty similar. And as long as I've known him, he hasn't ever wanted to get serious. That I know of, anyway. Until now."

"So you're saying he wants to get serious with me?" Why do I find it hard to believe a word he's saying?

"No, I'm not saying that."

"That's what it sounded like."

"I don't know what I'm trying to say." He pauses, and I hear his frustrated sigh. "Let me just put it this way. I've never seen him act like this over a woman before. Does that mean he wants to get serious? I don't know. I think he does, but that's just an opinion. Guys don't sit around and talk about that girly shit, you know?"

"No, I imagine they don't." I'm a little disappointed. I was so hoping he'd try to convince me or have some evidence to support his conjecture. But he doesn't. Cash is just as much a mystery to him as he is to everyone else.

Time to change the subject before I let the hands of this depressing funk pull me down into oblivion. Before I can think of anything to say, Gavin speaks.

"So, where does this mother of yours live?"

"Actually, she lives very near Carrollton, where I go to school. It's only about an hour from here."

"All right, west it is then."

As he guides his enormous vehicle toward the interstate, I think of something else to talk about.

"So, one of the many things you interrupted with your persistent knocking was the plan. Cash was just getting ready to tell me what he's going to do. Mind cluing me in?"

Gavin eyes me suspiciously. "Uhhh . . ."

"Who am I gonna tell? My mother? Like she'd care, even if I did. Which I wouldn't. I'm just concerned. That's all."

After another long pause, Gavin gives in. "He's going to make a couple copies of the video and keep them with different people. He's buying some ledgers that look like the books they want to take from him. Once he confirms the girl is alive and unharmed, he's going to show them the video. He'll explain that if they don't hand over the girl and ensure the safety of you and his father, both the video and the books will go to the authorities."

"Oh God! That sounds dangerous."

Gavin shrugs. "He holds all the cards right now."

"No, he doesn't. They still have Marissa."

"Okay, he holds *most* of the cards right now. If they don't hand her over, he'll give them the books. They'll be with Nash, who he'll call in *only* if things get crazy."

"So, he's hoping to get away with the books, the video, and Marissa?"

"Yeah."

"And worst-case scenario would be . . . ?"

"That he has to give them the books as an act of good faith to get the girl. But he'll still have the video and copies of the books. And whatever help Greg called in along with Nash."

"Greg? Is that Cash's father?"

"Yeah. He's a good man."

I say nothing. I still haven't decided if I think Cash's father is a good man or not. At the moment, I'd be more inclined to say not. He's the reason we're all in this mess to begin with. I'm sure he has some redeeming qualities; right now I just don't see them.

"Have you known him long?"

"Yeah, we go way back."

"I find that hard to believe. You can't be *that* old."

"I'm too hot to get old," he declares with a cocky grin and a wink. I roll my eyes and he laughs. "Nah, I started very, very early."

"Started what?"

He shrugs, but this time I think it's because he doesn't really want to answer, not because he's nonchalant.

"For a few years I was hired out to do all kinds of . . . odd jobs. But I can also fly planes and helicopters, which is how I met Greg. And then Cash."

I nod slowly. "Odd jobs, huh? So you're in a similar . . . business?"

"Not really. The work I did was dangerous and unsavory in a different way. That's why I got out."

It almost seems scarier to think what kind of person I'm riding with because he's so vague about what he does. Or what he *did*. And the way Cash talked about him, I can't help but wonder if I'm sitting next to a felon or something. Just because he's not in jail doesn't mean he's not guilty; it just means he never got caught.

All of a sudden, I'm much less curious about . . . everything! It seems that there's nothing but darkness and disappointment everywhere I look. For the first time in maybe *ever*, my mother's guest room is looking like a little slice of heaven.

EIGHTEEN

Cash

Letting Olivia go with Gavin was much harder than I expected. And now, as I guide my bike back toward the club, I keep thinking of what she looked like in my rearview mirror as I drove past her on the street. Very upset. She looked very, very upset.

I remind myself that Gavin is both trustworthy and capable. Doubting my judgment at this point would be as counterproductive as it would be stupid. There's nothing I can do about it. It's too late to make any big changes, especially ones that could risk Olivia. My gut was to go with Gavin. Now I have to trust it. Period.

Pulling into my garage and seeing the door to my apartment open reminds me I've got more problems than just worrying about Gavin's role in all this.

Nash.

I park the bike and walk in to find Nash in the bathroom shaving. After rinsing his cheeks, he meets my eyes in the mirror. I'm glad to see the hair of his goatee intact; I don't want him looking any more like me than he absolutely has to. This could get too sticky otherwise. Plus, I just don't like the guy.

"Make yourself at home," I bite sarcastically.

"Oh, don't worry. I did."

I don't even want to ask what that means. It'll just make me mad, and for the next twelve hours or so, I need to focus. And that doesn't mean on my brother.

"If you need to get a couple hours of sleep or do any more cleaning up, I can give you the keys to the apartment uptown and you can drive the car over there."

"Trying to get rid of me so soon?"

"Actually, yeah. I am."

"That's not very brotherly of you."

"Look, man, you're gonna have to leave the attitude at the door for a while. I don't have time for your mouth or your shit. Just stick to the plan and leave me the hell alone otherwise."

"Well, the plan includes a need for the video, which I've stashed in a safe place. I might take you up on the offer of the car. I don't have one, since I've been in exile for seven years."

Again with the bitterness. I want to roll my eyes, but I grit my teeth and resist the urge. Obviously one of us is going to have to be the coolheaded adult of the bunch. And it sure as hell doesn't look like it's gonna be Nash.

I walk into the bedroom and open the top chest drawer and

dig out my alternate set of keys. "Take the Beemer. The gold key is the one for the condo."

I give him the address. He raises his eyebrows and nods appreciatively, but he keeps his sarcasm to a minimum. I'm glad about that. Maybe I got through to him.

"Nice."

"Maybe for a lawyer, but I prefer this place."

He looks me in the eye, like he's trying to determine if I'm lying.

"I can't believe you did it."

"Did what?"

"Finished school and went to college. And actually graduated and became a lawyer."

I sift through his words for an underlying meaning, for derision or malice, but I find none. He just seems . . . surprised.

"It's not like I enjoyed it. That was always your thing, not mine. But it's what I had to do to help Dad. Or at least I thought it was."

I have to work to keep the bitterness from my own tone. It still stings knowing how much they kept me in the dark, remembering all the sacrifices I made because I thought Dad needed my help.

"I guess neither of us turned out quite like we expected."

"I suppose not. I just hope, in some ways, we're both better off for what we've done and the way things turned out. Maybe it was good for both of us. I needed a little bit of you, I guess."

Nash shrugs. "Maybe I needed a little bit of you, too. Just not this much."

His smile seems genuine, and it's easier for me to return it than I would've thought, considering how things started out between us.

Maybe there's hope after all.

I see Nash's few possessions thrown over the bed.

"I'll give you a minute to get your stuff together. I've gotta get something out of the car."

That's a lie. I actually have to get the books out of the safe and I don't want him to see where I keep important things. I still don't fully trust my brother, so I consider the fib prudent and necessary.

He nods and I walk back out to the garage, closing the door behind me.

I cross to the hook racks and pegboards on the wall opposite the car. There's a small lever and hidden hinges on the second board. It opens silently to reveal a safe built into the wall. I punch in the combination. The click lets me know it's ready.

The only things inside the safe besides the ledgers are an expandable file full of papers related to the club and a small stack of hundred-dollar bills. I hate not to have some cash on hand.

I remove the ledgers and shut the door, then replace the pegboard over it, concealing its presence perfectly. I retrieve my jacket from the backseat of the BMW and then head back to the apartment. Nash is putting on his sunglasses as I walk in.

"Seriously? At night?"

"All these years of the sun reflecting off the water has made my eyes sensitive to light. The glare of traffic lights at night bothers me. Plus, I look pretty badass."

His lopsided grin reminds me of the happy-go-lucky kid from our childhood.

"All you need is some leather pants and an Austrian accent and you could scare the shit out of some kids, Terminator style."

"In that case, I'm borrowing your bike for Halloween."

I smile but say nothing. That sounds an awful lot like he's planning to stick around, and I'm just not sure how I feel about that.

"One fright night at a time, man," I say lightly. "Let's get this one out of the way first. Can you be back here by eight or so?"

"Yep."

"And would you mind stopping by an office supply store on your way back and picking up some of these?"

I hold up the ledgers for him to see. He frowns and reaches out and grabs one. Flipping through the pages, he says quietly, "So this is what caused so much trouble."

"No. Dad's choices are what caused so much trouble," I say flatly.

Nash looks up at me. His gaze is hard, unyielding, but he says nothing, just hands me the ledger.

"I'll bring 'em."

"See you in a few, then."

And with that, he turns and walks out of the apartment.

NINETEEN

Olivia

With only about twenty minutes left before we get to her house, I brainstorm some sort of believable reason I'd be showing up on my mother's doorstep in the middle of the night. With a strange guy in tow.

It's been so long since I've called her, it takes me three tries to get the number right. It's programmed into my phone, but *my* phone is at Cash's apartment. I'm using one of the little cheapies that Cash wants me to toss in the trash every day or two.

My stepfather Lyle's sleepy voice sounds on the other end of the line. I breathe a sigh of relief. I didn't know any other number combinations to try, so I'd have been up the creek if this one hadn't been right.

"Lyle, it's Olivia. I'm sorry to call so late. Can I speak to Mom?"

I hear an exasperated sigh and some muffled sounds as he covers the mouthpiece with his hand. A few seconds later, my mother's voice comes on the line.

"Olivia, do you know what time it is, young lady?"

Leave it to my mother to be more concerned with propriety than the fact that her daughter is calling out of the blue at an ungodly hour.

"Mom, there was a gas leak at my place in town. Can I come stay the night with you?"

I hear a variety of noises before she speaks, none of which sound pleased. "Why aren't you staying with your father? Don't you have a key?"

"Dad broke his leg. It's hard for him to get around. Calling him in the middle of the night might cause him to hurt himself. So would just showing up."

Everything I'm telling her is true except the gas leak. "And I'm bringing someone with me. He's . . . well, he's a friend. I hope that's okay."

It's funny that I couldn't even force the lie that Gavin means something more to me. It seems that even my tongue is tied to Cash, which is freakin' ridiculous. But, knowing my mother, she'll make something else of it, anyway. She'll see and hear and perceive what she wants to and make all her judgments based on what's in her head. That's the way it's always been with her.

"If you think you're sleeping in the same room with this 'friend,' you can think again, Olivia."

I can almost see her lips thinning into a self-righteous pucker.

"I wasn't even going to ask, Mom. We just need a safe place. For tonight." Gavin pokes me, looking meaningfully at me. "A couple days at the most."

"A couple of days?" Oh yeah, she's outraged now. Inconveniencing my mother is a huge no-no.

"We won't interfere with any plans you've got. You won't even know we're there."

"I doubt that," she mumbles. "All right. When will you be here?"

"We're about fifteen minutes out now."

"All right."

With a click, the line goes dead. I sigh and hang up on my end. I look to Gavin and he grins.

"Sounds like a gem."

"Oh, she is."

Perceptive guy.

Just under twenty minutes later, Gavin is carrying my bag and following me up the long, curving, lighted walkway to my mother's front door. I stop on the stoop and take a deep breath, glancing at Gavin to my left. He's looking the house over, taking in the fancy brick exterior, the never-ending supply of windows and the expensive brass knocker attached to the huge wooden door.

"This ought to be interesting."

I smile. "Oh, you have no idea."

I knock.

Within seconds, the door swings open to reveal my mother, standing just inside, wrapped in a high-dollar silk robe. From her perfectly coiffed (yes, even in the middle of the night) sable hair to her sharp blue eyes to her thin arms crossed over her chest, she oozes disapproval. Essentially, she looks much like she did last time I saw her a couple of years ago. She's pretty much always disapproving. And she's pretty much always the same age. No doubt she spends thousands of dollars on preservatives. Eventually I'll catch up to her and we'll be the same age.

I wonder if they make any night creams laced with formaldehyde, I think obtusely as I take in her smooth, taut skin.

"Hi, Mom. Sorry to wake you."

She steps back and lets us into the foyer. "Not sorry enough, I see."

I resist the urge to roll my eyes. My mother has always been the type who can't let something go. She'll get something stuck in her head or fixate on a particular oversight and she'll beat it to a bloody pulp.

"I suppose not," I say agreeably. "We won't keep you up. This is Gavin. I'll show him to one of the guest rooms. I'll take the other. You won't even know we're here."

She *hmphs* and closes the door behind us. "You know the rules," she warns, looking pointedly at Gavin.

"I know, but I told you he's just a friend, Mom."

"I know that's what you *said.*"

This time I do roll my eyes. "Well, I'll see you in the morning. Night."

I reach for Gavin's hand and tug him forward.

As exhausted as I am, I'm having a terrible time getting to sleep. All I can think of are the things I didn't say. The things I didn't do or enjoy because of fear, because I don't trust myself. It was never about Cash and not trusting him because he's a bad boy. Yes, he is a bad boy. In some ways. But that's not the problem. Being a bad boy doesn't make him a bad person or a bad companion. But I couldn't see that past my own bias. I didn't trust my judgment. After making so many wrong decisions and letting my feelings blind me, I finally found someone worth loving and I froze.

And it couldn't have happened at a worse time.

Now I'm stuck with all the unsaid things, all the regret for having been afraid. For *not* having acted. Or spoken. Or jumped.

If, by some miracle of God, I get another chance before all this is said and done, I won't be such a coward next time.

TWENTY

Cash

I'm too jacked up on adrenaline to sleep. The closer dawn gets, the more anxious I get about how all this will go down.

I look at the clock. With no windows, I can't see the sun coming up, but I know it is. And it makes me think of Olivia, hopefully sleeping peacefully at her mother's house. Alone.

The thought of Gavin possibly curled up next to her makes me ill as hell. With a growl, I throw my arm over my eyes and try to clear my mind.

But it doesn't work. I can't stop thinking about her.

Maybe if I call and let it ring just once . . .

She isn't exactly a light sleeper. One ring shouldn't wake her if she's sleeping. But if she's awake . . .

I hit the key for the number of her disposable cell, and the phone automatically dials hers.

It rings once and I pause. Just before I hit the button to hang up, Olivia's hushed voice comes on the line.

"Hi," she says simply. I smile. I can almost see the shy look on her face as she says it. And in that one word, I can hear that she's pleased I called. Now I want to drive to her mother's house, sneak in the window, and have slow, quiet sex with her against the wall.

"You're awake."

"Yeah. Can't sleep. You, either?"

"Nah. My head won't shut up."

"I know the feeling."

There's a long silence, during which I'm sure she's wondering what it is that I want. Before I can speak, though, she does.

"I'm glad you called, actually. There's something I want to tell you. It's something I should've said earlier, but I didn't. I should've. And now I regret that I didn't. When we were face to face. But I'm an idiot, so . . ."

I smile into the dark. I'd be willing to bet a thousand bucks that she's fidgeting with her hair. She does that when she gets nervous. And it's very obvious now, by the speed of her rushed words, that she's nervous.

"What did you want to say?" I'm pretty sure I already know. I know how she feels about me. When she's not fighting it and not getting lost in the piles and piles of past shit that clog up her thoughts sometimes. And I would hope that, after everything that's happened, she knows how I feel. But she's a damn woman. I think they like having things spelled out for them.

Unlike men, they need the words, the definitiveness of them. Men don't. But I wouldn't mind hearing her say them, anyway.

I hear her deep breath and I imagine her squeezing her eyes shut like she's jumping off a bridge or something. Taking the leap. And, to Olivia, it probably feels like pretty much the same thing.

"I think I'm falling in love with you," she blurts. "Please don't say anything!" she hurries to say before I can speak. "I don't want you to feel obligated to say anything in return. I just didn't want to let you go into this without knowing how I feel, that I'm really trying to leave the past in the past and not let it get inside my head and screw things up between us."

"I don't feel obligated to say anything."

"Oh," she says, deadpan. "Well, good. Because I wouldn't want you to do that."

"I won't. If I tell you 'I love you' it's because I mean it, not because it's an expected response."

"Okay," she says quietly, then, "Oh crap! Mom's up. I've gotta go. Please be careful today!"

"I will."

"See you soon?"

"As soon as I know you're safe."

"Please let that be soon."

I laugh. "I'll do my best to make them bend to my will."

"That shouldn't be a problem. You're pretty good at that."

"How do you know?"

"You've worked your charm on me more than once."

"Baby, I haven't even *begun* to charm you yet. Just wait until you get back."

"I'll hold you to that," she murmurs, the smile evident in her tone.

"Damn straight. You'll hold whatever I tell you to, right?"

"Whatever you say, Colonel," she teases, referring to our banter when she thought I was Nash.

"Now that's what I like to hear."

"Maybe I'll even salute you when you come for me."

"I'll have the salute all taken care of. I'm sure there will be parts of me at perfect attention when I *come* for you."

"You're so bad."

"But only in the good way."

"Right," she says softly. "Only in the good way."

"Try to get some rest. I'll call when I get back."

"Okay. Talk to you then."

There's a pause. Neither of us wants to say the words. So we don't. She simply hangs up. And I follow suit.

TWENTY-ONE

Olivia

If ever there was a small hope I'd get some sleep, it's gone now.

Holy crap balls! I just told Cash I love him!

Well, sorta. Was what I said a cop-out? Was that the chickenshit's version? Probably. But at least he got the point before he goes off to make war with some mobsters. And that's what I wanted most—for him to know. My execution just sucked ass.

But that's not even the most emotional firework-ish part. That would be what he said to me afterward.

If I tell you "I love you" it's because I mean it, not because it's an expected response.

Did he tell me he loves me? Or did he tell me that if he loved me, he'd mean it? Or was he just giving me some background on his I-love-you MO?

What the hell?

The more I think about it, the more I go over each word, the more confusing it becomes.

On autopilot, I dress quickly and run a brush through my hair before I hit the door and head downstairs. The house is quiet, so I'm careful not to make much noise. Mom is an early riser. A very early riser. She likes her morning time to be peaceful, and my being here at all is one strike against me. I don't need to do anything more to poke the bear.

"Who dressed you? A six-year-old? Your shirt's on inside out."

I look down and, sure enough, my T-shirt is on inside out.

Autopilot, you suck!

I wave her off. "I didn't turn on the light. I'll fix it before anyone else gets up."

As if he's happy to make a liar out of me, Gavin chooses that exact moment to enter the kitchen.

"Morning, ladies," he says in his charming accent, his smile wide and pleasant. No one says anything for a few seconds, which doesn't seem to bother him one bit. "Olivia, I can see where you get your looks. You didn't tell me your mother's such a beautiful woman."

The urge to roll my eyes is strong. But then I start to feel sorry for Gavin. He is sooooo barking up the wrong tree!

"Another charmer, I see," my mother says caustically, eyeing Gavin with disdain. "Your wiles might work on my daughter, but you needn't bother with me. I'm all too familiar with your kind."

"My kind?" Gavin clearly has no clue what she's talking about. I probably should've forewarned him about Mom.

"Gavin, why don't you get your shower first? It won't take me long to get ready."

"Are we in a hurry?"

"Well, not really. My first class doesn't start for a while, but—"

"First class?"

"Yeah." At his blank expression, I continue. "Class. Classroom. College. You know, school, where I go to learn."

Gavin frowns. "But you're not going to class today."

"Um, yes I am."

"Um, no you're not."

"Um, yes I am. Why wouldn't I?"

He looks pointedly at me and then tips his head slightly toward my mother. He doesn't want to state his reasoning in front of her, but she totally misinterprets his action.

"Oh, don't mind me. She doesn't care what I think. Abuse her all you want."

"Abuse her?"

"You don't think keeping her from bettering herself is abuse? You don't think ruining her life with your mere presence is abuse?"

"How am I—"

"Mom, that's not what he's doing. Look, it's a long story. We can talk about it later. Right now," I say, looking pointedly right back at Gavin, "he's going for a shower while we have coffee."

I don't think Gavin particularly prefers the way I handled things, but he's smart enough not to argue in front of my

165

mother. I think he's catching on to the bug up her ass pretty quickly.

He nods slowly and starts to back out of the kitchen. "Yeah, I do need a shower. I have some phone calls to make, too."

After Gavin makes his uncomfortable exit, Mom and I are left with an equally uncomfortable silence. It's not empty, though. No, it's filled with all kinds of judgment and condemnation. She doesn't have to say a word. It's all right there on her face, plain as day, for all the world to see.

I sigh. "Mom, I know what—"

"Take my car," she interrupts me to say.

"What?"

"Take my car. Go on to school. Don't let that . . . person stand in your way. Be stronger than that, Olivia."

I won't even address the fact that she thinks I'm weak. She's never really tried to hide her opinion from me. Or anyone else who might be interested in listening.

"Mom, you don't know anything about Gavin. He's a really good guy."

"So you've said about all the other losers you've wasted your life chasing."

"I haven't chased them, Mom. And I haven't wasted my life. I'll be graduating soon."

"And then going back to help your father, wasting away on that farm."

"I don't consider that wasting away."

"Well, that's obviously a matter of opinion. But these boys

you keep latching on to. Olivia . . ." She shakes her head in exasperated disappointment.

"Mom, I may have made some poor choices in the past, but that doesn't mean that every guy who might share some of the same . . . characteristics I like in a man is the exact same kind of guy. It's possible to be a fun-loving person, but still be good and decent and kind."

"I'm sure it is. But you never seem to find that kind."

"I admit that I've not had great success in the past, but this guy is different, Mom. I can feel it."

"Are you saying you've never 'felt it' before? Because I specifically remember us having a similar conversation about at least two of your previous causes."

"They weren't 'causes,' Mom."

Arguing with her is exhausting.

"You called one of them a 'fixer-upper.' What is that if not a cause? You want to fix these bad boys, Olivia. You want to change them, make them into something you can live with. But that's never going to happen. Boys like that don't ever change. And certainly not for a girl."

"Some of them can."

"I'll believe that when I see it. When one of them proves his love to you, I'll never argue the point again. But until then . . ."

Until then, I'm just the dumbass that keeps falling into the same trap, over and over and over again.

"Do me one favor," she says, reaching across the island to lay her hand on mine, a rare show of affection and support.

"What's that?"

"Take my car. Go to school. Prove to me that you're strong enough to do this, strong enough to take on this kind of man and not buckle. Not give in and let him ruin your life. It would make me feel so much better."

Her expression is actually sincere. Maybe even a little worried and desperate. Does she seriously think that I'm so fragile and impressionable that I'll follow any ol' loser right over the cliff?

If I can do this one thing to prove to her I'm not the weakling she thinks I am, then why not? Maybe it would help things between us, and between her and Cash when she meets him.

When she meets him, I repeat in my head, hanging on to the thought that such a day will come.

"Okay."

"Okay what?"

"Okay. I'll take your car. I'll prove to you that I'm stronger than what you think. That I'm smarter than what you think."

She smiles, but it's more satisfied and smug than pleased and proud. It reminds me that no matter what I do, there's probably little chance of ever pleasing her. Yet I feel compelled to try.

"I won't even fuss about what you're wearing, but I do want you to turn your shirt right side out first."

"I will. Give me a few minutes. I need to brush my teeth and clean up a little better."

"That's fine. I'll get you the keys and you can leave whenever you want."

I nod and smile, trying not to think about how furious Gavin will be when he finds out I ditched him. It's not like it's a big deal, though. I mean, I'll be at school, surrounded by hundreds of witnesses. The only way I could be any safer is if I were hiding a ninja bodyguard up my butt.

Mom brings me the keys, then turns to the toaster and a bag of wheat bread lying to its left. Without so much as a word to me, she starts making toast, the same thing she's had for breakfast every day for the last thousand years.

Quietly, I slip off the stool and make my way back upstairs. Sometimes I wonder why I even care what she thinks.

I pause on the steps when I realize that what I'm doing has very little to do with what Mom thinks of me, or changing it. Things have been this way between us for years. No, this has everything to do with her trusting my judgment enough to see that Cash is a good guy, that I've finally found someone who's worthy in her eyes. I want her to see that. Not for my sake, but for Cash's. He doesn't deserve her bias. It has nothing to do with him and everything to do with my mistakes, her mistakes, and her inability to forgive or forget either.

My determination grows with my epiphany. Yes, I'll do this. And I'll show her that finding and dating Mr. Wrongs doesn't mean I'm incapable of finding Mr. Right. It simply means that I've had lots of practice learning to work my bullshit detector. If anything, I think that makes me a professional.

I snicker at my logic. And at the use of the term *professional*. Mom would die if she could hear my thoughts. She'd swear I'm a prostitute.

I'm looking at all this as a good thing. And the fact that I'm thinking of a future with Cash has to be a good sign. That means he'll get through this just fine and we'll have a chance to see where life takes our relationship. To me, it's worth exploring. Cash is worth any risk.

As I pass the guest bathroom, I hear the shower kick on. Gavin is just getting started. Quickly, I hurry to my room, grab my bag, and head for the second guest bath. I squirt toothpaste on my toothbrush, stick it in my mouth, and strip down before turning on the shower. I hate going anywhere without a shower. I can be in and out in a flash. If I dress at the speed of light, I can take my bag with me and put on some mascara and lip gloss on the way. I know that's frowned upon, but the roads should be fairly empty at this hour.

Blasting through a hurried hair wash, scrubbing my teeth as I rinse, and then hitting the high spots with my washcloth and a bar of Mom's expensive soap, I'm hopping out of the shower and toweling off before you can say *spit*.

I hurry to give my armpits a swipe with deodorant, give my neck a spray of perfume, and dress in the same clothes I wore for ten seconds this morning, only this time putting them on right side out.

"Can't be embarrassing my tight-assed mother, now can I?" I mumble to the mirror.

I push my feet into my shoes, throw my bag over my shoulder, and drag my fingers through the tangles in my hair as I tiptoe past the guest bath.

I pause to listen and can still hear the water running. I resist the urge to pump my fist. I'm not sure why, but I feel like I've just won some sort of competition worthy of headlines: "Ovaries Beat Out Testicles in Speed Shower Match."

I roll my eyes at my inane train of thought. I think my mother must've taken drugs when I was in utero. That's surely the only explanation.

I hit the stairs and don't stop until I'm pulling out of the driveway in my mother's Escalade. Less than thirty minutes later, I'm pulling into a parking spot outside the hall my first class is in. I don't want to go in too early, mainly because I'm not sure what time they open the lecture halls in the morning. I decide to break cover and call Ginger. I haven't talked to her since everything sort of . . . exploded.

Her voice sounds scratchy and groggy when she answers. "There better be a strip-o-gram on its way to me for a call this early. What the hell?"

I grin. "Wake up, sleepyhead. It's me."

That perks her up some. "Liv?"

"It's alive! It's alive!" I tease.

"If you promise not to like it too much, I'm gonna spank the shit out of you next time I see you. What time is it?"

"Too early for you to be up. Sorry, but I don't have much choice."

"It's never too early for you, my sweet." She partially covers her yawn. "Whose phone are you calling from? Did you find a third penis to add to the mix?"

"Oh God, no! Ginger!"

"What? I was just gonna congratulate you on your mad fornication skills. That's all."

"Uh-huh. Sure you were."

"Who am I to judge how you get your freak on? Just as long as you get it on."

"I don't have a freak to get on, Ginger."

"And that's a damn shame. One of those twins ought to be able to introduce you to your freak. Of course, if they need teachin', don't forget my number."

"Speaking of the twins . . ."

"Please, God, tell me that segue means you're about to give me details!"

"Um, no. But I do have something I'd like to run by you."

"Is it about dildo selection? Because those things can be tricky if you've never bought one before."

I sigh. "No, it's not about dildos. Do you always wake up this way?"

"Of course! Why wouldn't I? This is how I go to sleep. It just makes sense that I'd wake up this way. Awesome doesn't take a break, Liv. And it never sleeps."

I grin at that. "And neither does humility, evidently."

"Hey, I just tell it like it is."

"Then turn your brutal honesty this way for a minute."

"Okay. Whatcha got?"

I would never want to lie to Ginger, so I carefully avoid mentioning anything that might inspire her curiosity, especially about the whole twin thing. That could get ugly pretty fast.

I give her the short version (or should I say short*er* version) of the phone conversation between Cash and me. When I tell her what he said, her only response is really nothing more than a noise, but it still alarms me.

"Ahhh."

"What's that supposed to mean? 'Ahhh.'"

"Nothing. Not really. To me, it sounds like he was wussing out just as much as you did. It's not an outright declaration, but it's very provocative."

"Provocative?"

"Yes, provocative. As in to provoke. You know I'm a student of both provoking and being provoked, so I know."

"So I shouldn't take it as him telling me he loves me?"

"Just to be safe, I wouldn't. Besides, you don't want him telling you in that kind of situation, anyway. It makes it sound like he's just reflecting your sentiment. Surely a guy that hot can be a little more original."

"Oh he's original, all right."

"Damn you! Don't tease me like that unless you're bringing one of those bits of candy to my house right this minute."

"That would be difficult on a number of levels."

"Difficult? Difficult is breaking and entering. But for a piece of dick like that, I'd break so he could enter. I'd commit a felony and two misdemeanors for an hour with something like that."

"Just one felony? I think you're gonna have to up your game a little for these guys, Ginger."

A loud, dramatic sigh. "Fine. Three felonies, no misdemeanors, but that's my final offer."

"Sold!"

We both laugh, but then Ginger sobers. "Seriously, though, Liv, if you love him, I say take the risk, but I want you to be sure. He could tear your heart into a thousand tiny pieces if you let him."

"I know."

"But if he's the one, it would be worth it to try."

"I know that, too. And I think he is."

"And you should warn him that if he hurts you, I will scissor-kick him in the nuts. Tell him, okay? You tell him that. Because I mean it. I'll go all kinds of Bruce Lee on his tasty ass."

"I hope you won't have any reason to."

"Me, too, babe. Me, too."

"Well, it's—"

A knock on my window startles me and cuts off my next thought. My heart leaps into my throat for a second until what I'm looking at really sinks in. It's just a student. A young-looking guy wearing a Yankees ball cap and a white T-shirt with his backpack slung over one shoulder. He's smiling shyly, so I roll down my window to see what he wants.

"Can I help—"

Before I can even finish the sentence, a smelly rag is held tight over my nose and mouth. I struggle, but it makes no difference. Within seconds, the face in front of me swims sickeningly right before the world goes dark.

TWENTY-TWO

Cash

I'm standing in the parking lot of an old abandoned warehouse in the hell-if-I'd-be-caught-here-after-dark part of Atlanta. My instructions were to come alone to this address after I retrieved the ledgers from the bank. So I did.

Earlier, I made a show of leaving my apartment and going to a bank that I'm familiar with across town. I went back to where the safety-deposit boxes are located. The anteroom isn't visible from the rest of the bank, so I knew I could pull off my ruse from there.

There was a young, too-eager guy manning the desk outside that room. I talked to him about the rates for renting the boxes and how secure they are, shit like that to waste some time. I have no doubt they sent someone to follow me, so I was making it look good. I left the bank after about fifteen minutes, still carrying the bag I walked in with. When I got into the car, I slipped the fake ledgers into it, just in case someone got the wise idea of hijacking me on the way. But they didn't, which encourages me that they really might be willing to play ball.

Now, as I wait for . . . whatever to happen, my mind is on the empty ledgers in the car. Nash has the real ones. He's parked on the motorcycle behind an old generator a couple hundred feet away, watching.

I've been here for six minutes and haven't seen a soul. There's one rusty door to the right of the big hangar-style doors of the warehouse, but I haven't checked it. I'm not going into that building. They're batshit crazy if they think I'm dumb enough to do that. They can bring Marissa out to me.

I hear the crunch of gravel behind me, and I turn to see a white painter's van driving toward me.

Good God, could they be any more cliché?

It rolls to a stop near the building and a fat, balding guy in a track suit gets out of the driver's side.

Apparently, the answer is yes, they can be more cliché.

His back is to me, but I have no doubt that under the jacket of his black leisure suit is a wifebeater tank top and at least one gold chain around his neck. Evidently, the classic mobster look is no longer reserved for followers of *The Godfather* or *Goodfellas*.

I watch him walk across the gravel lot toward me. "Do you have the books?" he asks when he stops in front of me. His Russian accent is thick. *Do you have zee books?* It would be no surprise to anyone who knows organized crime that he's *Bratva*. Russian mafia.

"I'm sure you know I do."

Up close, I can see how this guy differs from movie mobsters. It's not his face. It's scarred, but not too grotesquely. It's not his size. His heft is intimidating, but not overly much, since I'm the same height and obviously in much better shape. It's not his words. They're direct and innocuous enough.

No, it's his eyes that make my palms sweat. They're cold and dead. If I ever had to describe to someone what the eyes of a killer look like, I'd describe these. Not the color or the shape, but what they say. They say he doesn't mind doing his job and that he probably never has. They're the eyes of someone who's never had a soul, someone who was probably born into this world doing horrible things to innocent people inside his head until he was old enough to do them in reality.

I pray to God these eyes never touch Olivia. Not even from a distance.

"Give them to me and I give you the girl."

"Let me see her first. I'm not giving you anything until I know she's okay."

Those eyes watch me for the longest ten seconds of my life before he speaks. Without fully taking his gaze off me, he turns his head and yells something in Russian. Seconds later, one of the van doors slides open and Marissa is pushed out of the van. Her hands and ankles are bound, and she's gagged and blindfolded. She falls limply to the ground, landing on her side.

I hear her moan of pain and see her draw her legs up toward her chest as if in pain. Around the gag and blindfold, I can see that her face is bruised, as is her shoulder, which is bared by the camisole she has on. It looks like the top to some pajamas I've seen her wear before. I hope they haven't done anything worse to her than just bruise her. Whether or not I really like Marissa or respect her as a person, I wouldn't wish what has happened to her on my worst enemy.

"Now, give me the books."

"Have them put her in my car."

"Show me the books first."

I had sort of figured it might go like this, so I feel prepared when I turn and walk to the car, retrieving the blank ledgers. I leave the driver's-side door open, which will hopefully save me valuable seconds if I need to get away quickly. I walk the books back to the big guy, stopping short of where I stood before. The more distance between us, the better.

I hold up the books briefly, then drop them back to my side. "Now, have them put her in my car."

The guy smiles the most chilling smile I've ever seen. It makes me wonder if I'm somehow playing right into his hands. I don't know how I could be, but I'm smart enough to know that underestimating people like this is a fatal error.

So I don't. I do my best *not* to underestimate him.

He calls behind him again, to whoever is in the van. "Duffy, put her in car."

I watch a smaller, more American-looking version of the

guy in front of me step out of the van, scoop Marissa up, throw her roughly over his shoulder, and carry her to the BMW. He opens the back passenger door and flings her onto the backseat. Through the still-open driver's side, I can hear her muffled sobs. I don't know if they're sobs of pain or relief.

"Now, give me books," he repeats, like I'm an obstinate child he's running out of patience with.

My heart tries to hammer its way past my ribs as I hand him the blank ledgers. As I suspected, he flips through them. When he raises his cold eyes to me, if possible, they're even colder.

"I thought you'd be smarter than this. Your father, not so smart. Look what happened to him." He pauses meaningfully. "And to his family."

Fire races along my veins at his reference to my mother and her horrific death. "Things are going to be different this time. You're going to let us leave here with the books and you're going to assure me, on behalf of you and your boss and all your shit-bag associates, that no one will ever come near me, my family, or my friends again. Because if you do, the books will be the least of your worries."

"What makes you think I do that?"

"Because we have video. Very damning video of the trigger-man at the dock that day seven years ago. A man who can be directly linked to Slava." Slava is the leader of the *Bratva* cell in the South. "Now I can promise you that as long as everyone I've ever known or met remains safe, this video will never see the light of day. But if—"

179

The cell phone in my pocket rings. My heart skips a beat. There's a problem. A big one. Everyone was clear on when to use this number—only if something has gone terribly wrong.

My stomach squeezes into a tight knot.

Olivia.

"Hold that thought. This must be my contact for getting you a preview of the video."

It's a bluff. Only Nash has seen the video and it's only on his phone, not mine. He made a copy onto a flash drive, but it's not with him. It's in a safe place, according to him. But it buys me a couple of minutes, which I apparently need.

"What is it?" I answer.

"They took Olivia." Gavin's words and the steel in his voice make my chest feel tight.

Holy shit, they've got her! Holy shit, holy shit, holy shit!

It's arguably my worst fear to date. And it's happening. Right now.

"Where?" I ask, mindful of the enforcer standing not too far from me.

"I followed them to a small brick house in Macon. Looks like a hideout."

"How the fu—" I catch myself, clamping my lips together tightly. I love Gavin like a brother, and I trust him. I trusted him with the thing most important to me. And he let me down. "What happened?" I ask, trying to be mindful of the people who might be listening.

"Took her mom's ride to school while I was in the shower." I'm too mad to respond. After a long pause, Gavin continues, his voice dripping with contrition. "Cash, mate, you know I'll do anything to help you get her back. I'm so sorry. I know—"

"Stop," I say, cutting him off. I don't doubt something unexpected happened, because he's still one of the biggest badasses I know, but at the moment I don't give a shit. I'm just angry at the fuckers who took Olivia. Furious even. And scared as hell. But there's no time for any of that. The only thing I care about is getting to Olivia.

"Are you . . . prepared?" I ask.

"Mate, I'm *always* prepared."

"I'll call you back."

My thoughts are racing through ways to get us out of this. Giving them another bargaining chip—the ultimate bargaining chip, as far as I'm concerned—was never part of the plan.

Outwardly casual, I smile at the big guy, turning just enough so that I can keep the smaller guy, Duffy, in my peripheral vision.

"Change of plans. I'll give you the books for the girl, but I'm holding on to the video as insurance."

"I don't think so. I don't believe you have video."

He takes a slow step toward me, one meant to be intimidating. And it is. I won't lie.

I take one step back.

"You'll get a preview of the video when you get the books, but the new deal is that you let us go and we can arrange another meeting for the video trade."

"Another trade? For what?"

"I know you took her." Even saying the words makes me

furious—at them, at myself, at my father. My pulse pounds in my ears, and my hands shake with the desire to tear into this guy.

His upper lip twitches.

"Give me the books *and* video or she's dead."

"No deal. It's my way or you'll never get what you want."

"No, it's my way or she dies." He takes another step toward me, only this one isn't slow. It's aggressive. I've made him angry. "And, just for the aggravation, I'll make it slow. I might even let some of these boys have fun with her before I kill her."

A blinding combination of fear and rage drops down over me. I can't think past the vision his words conjure and the fury and panic it inspires.

Before I can give the wisdom of it a second thought, my fist is flying through the air toward the big *Bratva*. It connects with his steely jaw and I hear a crunch. Whether his jaw or my hand, I can't be sure. I'm numb to any pain that I might otherwise be feeling.

He's so taken off guard by someone willing to actually touch him, he stumbles back two steps, giving me a momentary advantage. And I jump on it.

I come across with my left elbow, smashing it into his face as hard as I can. I push my position and keep pounding away at him—left, right, left, right, fist, fist, elbow, fist.

I barely hear the sound of the motorcycle approaching, and I barely feel the arm that wraps around my neck from behind and starts to squeeze. It's only when my air is cut off that I pause in my assault on the Russian. Duffy has me in a pretty tight choke hold.

Before I can throw him off, the big Russian plants one fist in my stomach, doubling me over. His knee meets my cheekbone next, knocking me to one side as light explodes behind my eye.

Blood is buzzing in my ears as I struggle to catch my breath. I'm gasping, staring at the ground, and I see the Russian's wingtips retreat one step. My head is getting fuzzy from lack of oxygen, and the only thing I can think of is that no one wears wingtips with a tracksuit.

My vision starts to blur when I hear the sound of a gun slide being drawn back to jack a round into the chamber. It's an ominous sound, but Nash's voice is even more so.

"Let him go or I'll put a bullet in your skull."

I know both of these guys have guns. My attack on the big one and the subsequent involvement of the little one served as the perfect distraction for Nash to move in and get the upper hand.

The grip around my neck eases enough that I can catch my breath. I inhale and straighten, expanding my lungs and gulping in air. After two deep breaths, my vision clears and I see the Russian glaring at me. His eyes aren't cold anymore. They're furious. And deadly.

"You boys, you make a big mistake," the big one says, wiping blood from his dripping nose and mouth with the back of his hand. Then, never taking his eyes off mine, he spits at my feet. "We don't bargain."

"That's funny because I was under the impression you brought me here today to bargain."

"I brought you here today to kill you," he says, deadpan.

"Not much of a negotiator, are you?"

"With one phone call, she'll be dead. Also, if I don't call with instructions within the hour, she'll be dead. No matter what you do, she'll be dead." My heart freezes inside my chest at the prospect. "Unless you give me what I want."

"You just said you don't bargain."

The Russian's sneer is nothing short of evil. "No matter. If you leave here today, I'll find you tomorrow. And her. And him," he says, tipping his head at Nash behind me. "You can't run far enough."

"I'd run that by your boss before you make any rash decisions. There's more than one copy of the video. Something happens to anyone I know and it goes straight to the police, along with some really helpful tips about the triggerman. And his associates."

A muscle in the Russian's jaw twitches as he listens to me. I can hear the heavy breathing of the little one, Duffy, at my back. Nash is behind us somewhere. The Russian's eyes have flickered over to him a time or two. I wonder if he knows who he is, if he recognizes my supposedly dead brother behind the facial hair.

"I still don't believe you. I think I kill you all and take my chances."

Suddenly, Duffy releases me and moves to the Russian's side. Turning to face us, he draws a gun from the waistband of his pants and trains it on me. I know I should be afraid, but it all seems so surreal, I'm just . . . not. My emotions haven't caught up with my brain yet. My adrenaline is still kicking the shit out of everything except for the fear that Olivia might get hurt. That's my primary concern right now.

I take a step back to align myself with Nash. I do a double take when I glance over at him. He's as pale as a girl under his tan, staring at Duffy like he's seen a ghost.

"What?"

"That's him," he says quietly, almost too quietly, like he's in shock or something. I just don't know why.

"That's who?"

"That's the bastard that killed Mom. He's the one on the video." There's about ten seconds of absolute silence while everyone digests what Nash said. He's the first to recover, of course. Taking us all by surprise, Nash lets out an animalistic growl and lunges forward. "You motherfu—"

With my reflexes still under the influence of an ass-ton of adrenaline, I'm able to reach out and stop him before he can get to Duffy. "Nash, no! They've got Olivia." I feel the muscles of his shoulder flex as he strains against me. When he looks at me, his eyes are blank. It's like he's so furious he doesn't quite understand what I'm saying. That or he just doesn't care. I give him a shake to snap him out of it. "They've got Olivia, man. Be smart."

His look assures me that *smart* to me is much different than what *smart* is to him. He's got no stake in this, only his hunger for revenge. That's all he wants. And I'm standing in the way

185

of that. But I'll be damned if I risk Olivia just to satisfy his needs. There will be time for that later, when we can think and plot and be prepared. Today is not that day. Today is only about making sure Olivia is safe. Nothing else. Nothing else matters as much. Not by a long shot.

I look to the Russian. "Still think we don't have a video?" If there were no video, Nash wouldn't have recognized the triggerman.

I can tell by the return of the tic in the big Russian's jaw that he doesn't like something. And I know exactly what it is. He's stuck. He knows there's no way he's leaving here with everything, and he knows he can't kill us and take it. So he has to bargain. Even though he says he doesn't bargain.

"You're not leaving here until I get the books. The *real* books."

I hate to give up the books, but the only reason Nash is here is so that I *could* give up the books without being up shit creek. And if this is the bone I have to throw these dogs to get them off my back so I can get to Olivia, so be it.

"Fine. Take the books. A good-faith offering." I turn and nod to Nash. His lips thin, and I can tell he doesn't want to give them a damn thing but a bullet between the eyes. I can almost hear Nash's teeth grinding. He looks livid. But he doesn't argue. Thank God. At least he didn't come back a total bastard. At least he can be considerate of the lives at stake here.

Never taking his eyes off the other two men, Nash reaches into the compartment behind the seat on the bike and pulls out the real ledgers. With an eff-you flip of the wrist, he flings the books onto the ground about a foot in front of the big Russian.

Still oozing blood from his nose and mouth, the Russian says one short, clipped foreign word to Duffy, who immediately moves to get the ledgers. He hands them over and the big guy flips through them, verifying that they're actually full of writing.

He opens each book and checks the front page, I assume for dates. When he gets to the third one, he turns to the middle of the book, then forward a few pages, scanning the rows of numbers for something. My guess is it's how he's authenticating that they're *the* books, not just any books or clever reproductions. This is exactly why I knew better than to try to deceive them. Mafia doesn't get to the level of criminal activity it gets to without having some brains.

When he seems satisfied, he looks up at me and sneers. "Take the girl in the car, but know that you've made enemies, enemies you don't want to make. This is not over."

With that, he nods to Duffy and the two turn and walk away, not the least bit concerned with turning their backs on us. I'm sure *they know* that *we know* that it would be suicide to do anything to them at this point, although I doubt Nash sees it that way.

When they're back in the van, I turn to Nash. "Take Marissa. I'm going to get Olivia."

"Bullshit! You're not leaving me with—"

"I don't have time for this right now. Get off my bike before I throw you off." One eyebrow shoots up like he might consider pushing me just for the hell of it, but then he sighs and gets off the bike. "Keep your phone on. Marissa will tell you where to take her." I sling gravel all over the place as I peel out and gun it. Once I get to a more populated street, I pull over and call Gavin.

"Where the hell are you?" he asks without preamble.

"I'm on my way. Give me directions." Gavin gives me the route he took to get to the house and describes which one it is. "Do you know how many people there are inside?"

"From what I can tell, just the two who took her. One young guy, one old. Now that you're on your way, I'll sneak out and see if I can get close enough to have a look around. When you come, stop at the north end of the street and walk in. There are some trees that can keep you from sticking out like the giant bloke you are."

"I'll be there as soon as I can."

"Be careful. Somebody's gonna have to get her the hell out of there while I clean up the mess."

That tells me all I need to know about Gavin's intentions.

TWENTY-THREE

Olivia

It wasn't a dream. I realize this with a fuzzy sense of panic as my hearing comes back online like a flickering fluorescent bulb. I recognize the voices I'm hearing. They're the same two I heard earlier. How much earlier, I don't know. Time has slipped away from me altogether.

"She's waking up again," I hear one say. "Give her some more."

I try to shake my head and tell them not to, but the slightest movement sends a sharp pain lancing through my skull and saliva gushing into my mouth. I hear a moaning sound and realize it's me. That must be what the *no* that's in my head sounds like out in the open air.

"Hurry before that bitch starts screaming again."

I try again to dissuade them, but I hear only a garbled gurgling noise.

My head spins and dips, even though my eyes are closed. The slow squish of blood through my veins sounds like a tired river inside my skull. I try again to speak. "Nooooo morrrrrrre." The words are drawn out around a protracted moan.

What's wrong with me?

"Pour some more on the cloth and hold it longer. Maybe you're not giving her enough."

I whimper. I can't help it. I know instinctively that they shouldn't give me more. I feel like I'm barely hanging on as it is.

"Too much," I slur.

One lowers his voice, but I can still hear him. "Is she supposed to sound like that?"

"I don't know."

"You don't think that elbow to the head did something to her, do you?"

Elbow to the head?

Fear brings just enough adrenaline with it to clear my head of the fog that muddles it. At least a little.

I think back to the parking lot at school. I remember rolling down my window. I remember the cloth over my face. But then there's a blank until I was being carried. Disjointed images from the underside of a bridge flash through my mind, and I remember waking up as the two guys were transferring me into another vehicle. I remember kicking and screaming, clawing and biting until the one holding my upper body dropped me. I screamed and kicked harder with my feet until something dense and heavy hit me upside the head. And then there's nothing again until I woke up tied to a bed in an otherwise empty room. I raised my head and started to look around just as the same young guy lunged at me with a rag in his hand. He smothered my face with it until blackness swallowed me again.

That's the last thing I remember until now.

"We're not supposed to kill her yet. Maybe just give her a little bit more, in case we need to wake her up and let someone talk to her or whatever."

"Yeah, let's do that."

I feel tears running down my cheeks, but it's an oddly detached sensation, like I'm feeling the warm streaks through a layer of fabric stretched over my skin. I try to open my eyes to see what's going on, but they won't cooperate. It's a struggle just to draw one breath after another. My chest feels so heavy, the urge to sleep so very strong.

The strength to fight eludes me when I feel the rag come across my face. I try to turn my head away, but the hand is persistent and I'm too weak. Vaguely, like smoke drifting through a room, it occurs to me that they might be giving me enough of whatever they're using to cause permanent brain damage. I think of Dad and how heartbroken he'll be. I think of Mom and how smug she'll be. But most of all, I think of Cash. Of what his lips feel like, what his smile looks like. Of all the things I didn't say, of all the things I'll never get the chance to say now. Of how cowardly I was about telling him I love him. More tears course down my cheeks, fading, fading, fading until I feel them no more.

And then all thought is gone.

TWENTY-FOUR

Cash

I know that on top of the twenty or so traffic laws I've broken, I've also just been plain dumb. I don't think I've ever made it across Atlanta faster, and during a busy time of the day, too. Weaving in and out of the flow, taking to the shoulder and emergency lane dozens of times to get around clogged spots, squeezing between cars to get through a slow place—none of it has been advisable. Getting myself killed trying to get to Olivia won't do anybody any good. But still . . . that doesn't seem to matter. All I can think of is what they might to do her, what they might've *already* done to her.

I grit my teeth against the rage that floods my bloodstream. If they've laid a hand on her . . . If they've harmed so much as one hair on her beautiful head . . . God forbid, if they've done things to her . . .

Just the thought of the twisted things men like this do to women makes me feel both sick and furious. I comfort myself with the thought that they haven't had her very long. By the time I get there, it should be a couple of hours at the most. But to Olivia, the captive, that could feel like a lifetime.

And it's all your fault for dragging her into your mess to begin with.

I twist the handlebar and throttle up even more, as though it's possible to outrun my mistakes if I drive fast enough. It's not, of course. There's nothing I can do to reverse the damage. My only hope now is to fix it for the future. To make it so that she's never in danger again. Even if it means becoming a criminal to do it.

It goes against everything I am now, everything I believe in to turn in that direction. But I can say that I have a better understanding of my father's motives now. Everything he did, he did for us. Even if it was incredibly stupid. I guess it's just a matter of finding something or someone worth going to such extremes for.

Like Olivia.

Again, like a nightmare you can't forget even after your eyes are open, I picture her screaming as faceless men torture her, tear at her clothes, touch her with their grimy hands. That's when all my convictions go straight out the window. I would have no problem whatsoever taking the life of someone who would hurt her. None. I might live to regret it, but if it meant keeping her safe, my regret would extend only so far.

The pit of my stomach churns with anger. My teeth grind with rage. My jaw aches from being clenched so tightly. Fury, like an uncontrollable animal, claws at the inside of my chest, desperate to get out and take its revenge.

Cranking the throttle even higher, I speed toward Olivia.

The rest of the short drive goes by in a blur of violent thoughts and horrific imaginations. By the time I drive past the street Gavin specified, I feel like I might explode if I don't get my hands on someone, someone to pound my fists into until they're lifeless beneath me.

Parking my bike behind a red minivan, I walk casually down the street until I get back to the intersection just beyond where they're holding Olivia. I stop at the stop sign and look both ways, taking in as much detail as I can without seeming suspicious.

The street looks innocent enough. It's a lower-income neighborhood. That much is obvious by the size and simplicity of the houses. Two fairly neat rows of small, square, shutterless brick homes line the street. The lawns are neat but functionally so. There's no fancy landscaping here. There are a few bikes on a few walkways, but I don't see any elaborate outdoor equipment in any of the backyards.

As I make my way along the cracked sidewalk that snakes between overgrown trees, I realize it's the perfect place to be anonymous. There are a few cars along the street, likely those who work the night shift and are sleeping by now. The rest of the residents are probably either at work or at school, leaving the criminals with lots of privacy to do whatever they like. There's no one around to hear any screams.

I spot Gavin's Hummer. My eyes scan the area from left to right as I approach it. When I confirm that it seems we're not being watched, I open the door and duck inside.

Immediately, Gavin hands me a knife with a four-inch blade, perfect for cutting throats or stabbing into deep tissue. Without question, I take it and slide it into my boot as Gavin screws a silencer onto the end of a Makarov.

"Irony?" I ask, referring to the Russian-made gun. Gavin grins. "So, what do you know?"

"Not much more than I did. With the houses like this, and it being daylight, it makes it hard to sneak around. Now if I'd known and could come prepared, I'd be checking the cable or telephone. But as it is, I'm lucky I had my stash with me."

"Thank God you're a paranoid bastard."

"Right. Otherwise your girlfriend might be in deep shit."

"You mean deeper shit."

"Well, I figure it could've been worse. The blokes that have her shouldn't be too much of a challenge. I'd say we got lucky the transaction with you was going down at the same time. If I had to guess, they'd made all kinds of preparations for that. Not just making the trade, but disposing of bodies as well. All in all, I think we're in good shape. It doesn't hurt that they're *Bratva*, either. No one should find out about what's going to happen in that house until some of the big boys come to check in on these pissants when they don't answer the phone."

It helps that this is probably the kind of neighborhood where people mind their own business.

"You've been here all morning. Don't you think this is pretty risky, considering someone may have gotten your license plates?"

"Nah, I circled the block when I saw them stop and stuck one of my stolen sets on. They're magnetized, so they just slide right over the real plates and no one's the wiser. *If* anyone gets my tags and *if* the police somehow get involved, they'll have the plates of an old pedophile who lives in Canton." He pauses and frowns, nodding. "Actually, it might be a good thing if someone *does* get the number. I think that bastard needs a little visit from the authorities right about now."

"So what are you thinking, then?"

At the thought of taking action, adrenaline pours into my bloodstream. I feel like I could bench-press a damn car!

"You're not anxious to get in there, are you?" Gavin teases.

I think of Olivia and I grit my teeth. "I can't wait to get in there and crack some skulls. If they so much as laid a finger on her . . ."

My heart pounds in my chest as I try to push visions of a brutalized Olivia out of my head.

"You just have to stay calm, Cash. We have to make sure to do this right or bad things could happen."

I take a deep breath and nod. "I know, I know. I'm not worried about them hurting me. I just want to get her out safely. I don't give a shit what happens to them, as long as they never come after her again."

I look at Gavin, and he's shaking his head. "Ever," he says with finality. It's not a little thing, what he's saying. We stare at each other for a tense second or two, and then I nod in agreement.

"Ever."

Another gush of adrenaline, possibly mixed with a little fear of what might be ahead. I'm not afraid of the people themselves. Or even really getting Olivia out safely. I *will* get her out. And I *will* make sure she's safe. There is no other option.

It's the consequences I'm afraid of. I've seen up close and personal what can happen when plans go awry in dealings with people like this. It's not pretty. It's ugly. In fact, it's often ugly to the tune of twenty-five years, if not a grisly death.

"Then let's go get this done. Why don't you drive me around the block and drop me off? Come back and park somewhere else. You go to the front door and I'll go to the back. I'm sure there's a back door."

"You might run into a little something back there. Don't forget that they've probably been warned."

"They shouldn't have any idea that I know where they're at, though."

"No, but they've probably already gotten a call that the plans have changed. They might be getting ready to move her or do . . . something to her."

I feel a knot of pure hell lodge in my throat. "Then let's get in there."

Gavin starts the Hummer and shifts into gear. "Lift up the backseat. I put a storage space under it. There should be some hats and gloves and face paint. It's not like going in under the cover of night, but at least we can disguise our features a bit." I reach back and lift, but the seat won't budge. "There's a little lever under the cushion."

Feeling for the lever, I find it and press it as I lift. The rear cushion folds up to reveal a small storage space. Sure enough, there are a couple of hats, gloves, and face paint, among all sorts of other needful things.

"My best friend is a guerrilla," I say caustically, taking out what we need.

"You better be glad, too."

I snap the seat back down into place and turn toward the front. I look at Gavin, he glances at me, and I nod. "I am, man. I appreciate it more than you'll ever know." Gavin nods, too. I know he knows how sincere I am. It's there in his expression. It's kind of like a brotherhood we're in. We have pasts we're trying to escape, we're both willing to go to extreme measures for those we care about, and we'll both likely meet an early death. That's a lot for a couple guys to bond over. It's a tighter friendship than any number of football or frat parties can make.

I pop off the flat, round lid of the dish of face paint. The content is inky black and looks like shoe polish, only oilier. Flipping down the visor, I quickly rub two fingers through the grease, then smear streaks of it on my cheeks. I repeat the action until my features are patchy and less discernible in the mirror.

I shove the ball cap onto my head and pull it low over my eyes, then push my hands into the gloves. Gavin slows to a stop on the street behind the house.

"I'll whistle when I get to the porch. Keep your head down and your hands in your pockets. Don't forget to watch your flank. Be careful in there."

"Thanks, man. You, too."

"I'll leave the keys under the floor mat. Get Olivia the hell out of here as soon as you can."

"Here," I say, taking my motorcycle keys out of my pocket and handing them to Gavin. "Behind the red minivan, one street over. Meet you back at my place." I reach for the door handle. "See you on the other side." Gavin smiles and holds up his fist. I give it a bump before stepping out of the Hummer.

Keeping my chin tucked against my chest and my hands in my pockets, I make my way slowly across the sidewalk to the house that sits behind the one where they're holding Olivia. Casually, I walk through their yard and around the side of the house, steadily approaching my destination.

I hear the throaty grumble of the Hummer as Gavin drives by the house to park down the street. I slow my pace enough to give him time to get to the front door. I stop to pretend to tie my shoe, which makes no sense because I'm wearing boots. But it looks good if anyone's watching from a distance, which hopefully they aren't.

I hear the clap of Gavin's boots on the sidewalk, followed closely by some light whistling. I rise and walk to the back patio, stepping onto it and approaching the door. It's old and wooden and looks easy to kick in.

I hear the doorbell ring, and then I hear a couple of hushed voices followed by some footsteps. Just out of curiosity, I try the doorknob. It's locked.

No such luck. That shit only happens in the movies.

When I hear the first sign that Gavin has made his move, which in this case is a guy yelling, "What the hell?" I raise my leg and kick as hard as I can just below the doorknob.

As I suspected, this place being an older home, the door frame gives way easily and the door pops open. Standing in the kitchen, watching with a stunned expression as I step through the wreckage that used to be the back door, is one of Olivia's captors. He's a young, college-age guy, but that doesn't make me feel the least bit guilty for beating the shit out of him.

He doesn't even see my fist coming.

Two punches to the face and he's unconscious.

That was easy enough.

I step over his body, sparing a glance toward the front door, where Gavin is pummeling another of the *Bratva*'s boys. Seeing that he's very much in control of the situation, I start looking for Olivia.

There's a short hallway to my right. It's lined with three closed doors. She could be in any of them. At the end of the hall is either another door, a closet of some sort, or possibly stairs to a basement. Hurriedly, I open the first door I come to.

I see only a flash of movement before he's on me. I take a

punch to the gut before I recover enough to smash my fist into his balls. I hear his groan and he falls at my feet. I kick him in the ribs and then kneel to punch him once in the face. His head lolls lifelessly to the side. I give him another hit just to make sure he'll stay down.

Obviously there are more here than what Gavin thought.

I look around the small bedroom. It's empty but for a beat-up green recliner and a television sitting on an old plastic crate. I exit the room and proceed to the next door, using a little more caution.

I twist the knob, push open the door, and step back. I hear the gunfire a millisecond before I feel the bullet graze my shoulder. It's not enough to stop me, though. The next one, however, nicks my ribs on the left side. It slows me down and hurts like a son of a bitch, but it's not enough to keep me from launching myself across the room at the guy before he gets off another shot.

We crash to the ground, my hat flying off as I use all my weight to roll him over, which isn't easy because this scarred bastard is much bigger than the others I've seen. As soon as I have the dominant position, I slam the crown of my forehead into his nose. Above the roar of my pulse, I hear the crunch of bone as the guy yells in surprised pain.

Before he can fight back, I see Gavin's boots appear at the top of the man's head. Then he's bending down to wrap the crook of his elbow under the guy's chin and squeeze. The *Bratva*'s hands go straight to Gavin's thick arm to try to free himself. Ineffectively, I might add. Gavin's strong as an ox and twice as mean if you're on his bad side. And this guy? He's on the bad side.

Levering myself up off him, I nod to Gavin and head for the door. Only two more rooms to check for Olivia. She has to be here somewhere.

TWENTY-FIVE

Olivia

As I begin to come awake, I hear a loud pop followed by some banging against the wall. I know where I am, inasmuch as I'm being held captive . . . somewhere. And in a fuzzy, disjointed way, I remember immediately the fear that gripped me when the rag was placed over my face again the last time.

I recognize the noise as gunfire. I know it's strange, but my initial reaction isn't fear; it's relief, relief that I can put the sound together with its source, that I can quickly make the association.

That must mean my brain is still working to some degree. I'm not a cucumber yet.

I hear a second shot. It brings with it a more logical response. Fear. No, not fear. Terror. My pulse races with it. The sensation is only exacerbated by the fact that I can barely move, much less do anything about whatever is happening. I realize I'm helpless and that my fate will likely be decided without my even being able to manage coherent speech.

Where's Ginger when I need her?

In my head, I'm laughing. As a bystander might, part of me is worrying that I'm making light in the midst of such a serious situation.

Am I losing it? Is any of this even real?

I struggle to open my eyes. Blearily, I blink my reluctant lids. A bright reflection on the ceiling swims across my vision, making my stomach roil. I close my eyes for a single breath and then fight to open them again.

I hear bumping again and the sounds of heavy footsteps. My heart thumps heavily inside my chest as panic sets in.

They're coming for me! Oh sweet God, they're coming for me!

Summoning every bit of strength left in my sedated body, I lift my head off the flat, smelly pillow and look from left to right. I'm in a small, sparsely furnished bedroom. Alone. With a window to my left.

I don't feel the tears so much as see my vision blur behind them. If I could just make it to the window . . . and outside . . . to freedom . . .

Maybe someone would help me . . .

Taking a deep breath, I bend my arms and slide my elbows under me to try to push myself into a somewhat upright position. As though they're made of jelly, though, they melt away as soon as I try to bear any weight on them. I try a second time, to no avail.

The futility of my efforts, the hopelessness of my situation hits me hard again. Only this time, the longer I'm awake without the drug-dosed rag being shoved in my face, the clearer my head becomes. And the more panicked I feel.

I'm telling myself I'll try again and again when a loud crash sounds at the door across the room. Splinters fly when it's torn off its hinges by a body being launched through the opening. My mind struggles to take in what I'm seeing.

A man I've never seen before—tall and with a springy bush of brown curls on his head—lands with a thud on the floor in front of the bed. I look back to the doorway, my heart lodged in my throat, and I see the most wonderful hallucination I could ever imagine conjuring.

It's Cash, standing like a thundercloud, right in front of me. His face is smeared with black streaks and his lips are curled in rage. He looks fierce. He looks murderous.

He looks like heaven.

For a fraction of a second, his eyes lock with mine. I see the anger, the determination, the I'm-teetering-on-the-threshold-of-apeshit-crazy. But I also see relief and something that makes my heart swell. Then his attention moves to the foot of the bed.

I see him drop to his knees and I hear his animal growl as his fist pumps up and down over and over again. The dull thump-squish-crunch makes saliva gush into my mouth. The image that comes to mind is of a bloody, mangled face being pounded into the floorboards by Cash's massive fist. But I can hardly feel sorry for the guy. In fact, if I could manage to move, I might go lend a hand in beating the ever-lovin' crap out of him.

Just a few seconds later, Cash is coming to his feet and rushing to the side of the bed. The whole scene has a surreal quality until he squats down, putting his face level with mine, and reaches out to gently touch my cheek with his fingertips.

"Are you okay?" he whispers. His face is a mask of agony. I can see the guilt eating at him. He thinks all of this is his fault.

"I am now."

He closes his eyes for a heartbeat. When he reopens them, his soul is there for me to see. "Oh my God, Olivia, I didn't know . . . I thought . . . If something had happened to you . . ."

"I'm fine," I say, not really knowing whether I actually am. I just feel the overwhelming need to soothe Cash and take away some of his pain.

Right before my eyes, I see logic sweep in and force him into action. "We have to get you out of here."

I know he's right and I can feel the medication wearing off a little more every minute, but still, I don't think I can walk.

"Can you help me up?"

A frown flickers across his forehead. "Help you up?" he asks, almost like he's insulted. I feel confused, but he doesn't give me time to ask questions. Rather, he rises and slides his hands beneath me and lifts me into his arms.

As though I've been given a sedative, a drug of a different kind, being in Cash's arms has an instant and an intense effect on me. I feel like crumbling and flying, like dancing and crying, like living and like dying. Wrapped up in him, in his bad-boy ways and his good-guy heart, is my whole world. Somehow, while I wasn't looking, I fell. And I fell hard.

For my soul mate. For the love of my life. For my hero.

In the blink of an eye, I realize I've never been broken by a bad boy. I've never been devastated by a cheater. I've never been duped by a player. I've never cared enough for them to do me any real damage, any lasting harm. My pride has been wounded, my heart has been kicked around a little and my self-esteem has taken a hit or two, but all that's like child's play in light of what the loss of Cash could do to me.

What I did learn from my relationship failures, however, is that trust doesn't come easy for me. I've blamed my issues on the men in my life. I've chalked every disastrous attempt at love up to the skirt-chasing ways of the bad boy, when it's been me all along. Subconsciously, I've chosen men who would prove me right about the worthlessness of a bad boy, rather than bring to light my own shortcomings, my own fears. And it's been a convenient cop-out until Cash came along. Cash broke all the rules, broke all *my* rules. He's not giving me reason to run. He's giving me reason to stay. And all I have to do is muster the courage to do it, to take the chance that it *might not* work out, to take the chance that I may very well get hurt. He's giving me something to invest in, and all I have to do is believe in it.

For real this time.

But can I take the leap? Can I tell him I love him, and mean it, when death isn't knocking at my door? When disaster isn't looming? Can I open up my chest and make my heart vulnerable to him?

In the space of a heartbeat, with Cash looking down into my face, I've worked my befuddled mind into a twisted maze of confusion and uncertainty. With a small smile of gratitude, I lay my head on his chest and let him carry me from the room. There will be time for thoughts and musings and declarations later.

I hope.

I feel his lips brush my hair and I hear his sigh whisper through his chest just before he whisks me away. In three long, powerful strides, he crosses the room and carries me out into the hall. He pauses at the first doorway to look inside, then does the same at the second. When he finds it empty as well, he puts his back to the wall and creeps toward the light shining at the end of the short passageway.

Gavin rounds the corner, startling a surprised chirp out of me. His face is done up much like Cash's, the dark paint making his blue eyes pop. They're not the sexy, twinkling blue eyes I've come to expect, though. These eyes are cold and serious and . . . ominous. It's almost like seeing another personality living behind the familiar face.

"She all right?" Gavin asks of Cash, tipping his head at me.

"I think so. I'll check her out when I get her home."

"I won't be long. I just have some . . . cleaning up to do."

Without another word, Gavin moves into the room at my

right, takes a fallen man by the hands, and begins to drag him toward the hall. Cash walks ahead of him, aiming for the door. I watch Gavin over his shoulder.

He pulls the unconscious man into the main living area, the floor of which is devoid of any kind of furniture but for a single old, brown couch. He deposits the man at the end of a row of bodies. Each one is lined up next to the other, shoulder to shoulder, like a bizarre prone firing line. A shudder passes through me as I wonder at their fate. It's in that moment I realize that, despite my animosity toward them for holding me against my will, I really don't want to know what's to become of them. I have a feeling I'll be better off without that kind of information.

Outside, Cash pauses on the front porch, looking left and right. When he spots what he's looking for, he starts off down the street at a fast pace, even for his long legs. I see Gavin's Hummer come into view just before I hear the beep of the keyless entry. Quickly, Cash opens the passenger-side door and, with such excruciating tenderness that it tears at my heart, sets me on the seat and buckles me in.

He raises his head and gazes into my eyes. He looks tired yet relieved. He gives me a lopsided grin. "Rest, baby. You're safe." With a brush of his lips over mine, he closes the door. I'm asleep before he even gets behind the wheel.

TWENTY-SIX

Cash

Irritated, I grip the steering wheel a little tighter.

I sound like a damn woman!

We've been on the road long enough that the adrenaline has faded and my thoughts have turned completely toward Olivia. I bet I've glanced over at her sleeping face thirty times since we left. Maybe more. That number might be a little conservative.

It's just that she looks so beautiful and the sight of her is so . . . welcome. Although I refused to think about not being able to get her out of this mess alive and well, on some level I must've been worried about it. Now all I'm doing is bouncing back and forth between being thankful that she's all right and vowing that I'll never let anything happen to her.

Today was the first step in ensuring that. With Nash's video, we've bought some time. Gavin is taking care of the lower-level threats and sending a very effective, if dangerous, message. Next up is taking care of the big guns and making sure that no one ever has reason to come after Olivia again, unless they're willing to risk severe consequences.

I'm still hoping the second ad I placed, the second ace up Dad's sleeve, might give me something else to work with. If not, I'll just have to make do with what I've got until I can come up with a plan. Now that Olivia's safe, I ought to be able to concentrate a little more effectively.

Just thinking of her draws my eye back to the passenger seat, where she's resting peacefully beside me. I reach out to touch her hand but pull my fingers back before they can graze her skin. I don't want to wake her up.

But damn, I want to touch her!

It feels almost like a compulsion, to touch her and make sure she's really with me and that she's really safe. And that's ridiculous, too.

Good God! I'm gonna wake up with ovaries if this shit doesn't stop!

The thing is, I don't know how to stop it. I've never wanted to feel this way about a female. And even now, I'm not sure I do. But I'm also not sure I have a choice. It's almost like Olivia's cast some sort of spell on me. And I don't like feeling this way—this helpless, this invested, this . . . emotional. I don't ever want to lose myself in a woman.

Ever.

With my teeth clenched in determination, I keep my eyes facing forward. On the road. Not on Olivia.

Olivia is sleeping soundly in my bed when Gavin returns almost two hours later. We go out to talk in the office, where we won't disturb her.

"How's she doing?"

"She's been sleeping. I'm sure she's exhausted."

"We all are, mate. You especially. You look like shit."

"Thanks, Gav. I can always count on you to say things that help me in *no way whatsoever.*"

His grin is the same caliber as any other day—carefree. It's his ability to cope with the things he's done (and *still* does occasionally) that makes him so good at his job. He sees the world as black and white, good and bad, live or die. He's a good guy. Really, he is. It's just that he doesn't tolerate criminals very well, even though that's how every law enforcement agency in the entire world would label him. I mean, I'm not going to sugarcoat it. Gavin is a former mercenary, a hired gun. A killer. It's just that he's a killer with a conscience. And God help your soul if you happen to step on it the wrong way.

"I just call 'em like I see 'em," he says, laying on thick his best impression of a Southern accent.

"How'd it go? Any problems?"

He flops down in the chair behind the desk, rests one ankle on his knee, and laces his fingers behind his head. "No. Two to the head of each. The message ought to be pretty clear."

I nod. I don't really know what to say. What he did for me, for us, for *Olivia* was more than I could ever have asked him to do. And yet he did it, anyway. He was there when I needed him, without question, without reservation. Gavin's probably one of the few people in the world I can fully trust. As of right now, we've been through too much together to be anything less than brothers. "Thanks, man. I can't tell you . . . . I just . . . ."

"I know, mate. I know," he says soberly. He clears his throat, then changes the subject. "I called the mother."

"What?"

"I had to. Her daughter went missing. In her car. I had to tell her Olivia was in danger in order to get her to tell me where she went and what she was driving."

"Oh my God," I say, dragging a hand over my face. "What did she say?"

"At first I don't think she believed me. That lady's a piece of work. I think she thinks all men are controlling and she tries to turn Olivia against anyone she brings home. Or at least that's the impression I got."

"Maybe it was just you. Ever think of that?"

"Are you kidding me? With this face? Mothers love me. And I mean *really* love me," he says with a wicked grin. And I'm sure he's right. By most anyone's standards, Gavin is a good-looking guy. Add to that his charm and his accent, and the ladies go wild. But I couldn't care less as long as it's not Olivia going wild over him.

"What'd you tell her?"

"I told her Olivia was safe and that the Escalade had been dumped under the bridge at the overpass just off campus."

"Great! Now she'll go straight to the cops."

"No, I told her that's the worst thing she could do, that it would only draw the attention of these people toward her. Trust me, she doesn't want that. And I think she understands that. She's got a lot of selfish bitch in her. She probably wouldn't have listened to me if I hadn't put it to her that way."

"Well, as long as she doesn't do anything stupid."

"You'll just have to . . . reiterate the importance of leaving the cops out."

"*I* won't be reiterating *anything*. Why would I need to call her after you did? I've never even met the woman."

"You don't need to call her. She'll be here to check on Olivia tonight. After she gets everything straightened out with her SUV."

"She's coming here?" My voice is unnaturally high in my shock.

Gavin grins. "Damn, did someone just punch you in the nuts? What was that?"

"Not yet, but if what Olivia says about that woman is accurate, she'll probably be grabbing herself a fistful while she's here. And not in the way *you* were talking about."

"Trust me, you don't want that woman touching anything below your waist. Ever. For any reason. That sheila could make a man's body parts shrivel up and fall off. Hypothermia."

"And she's coming here." Not that I'd ever really *wanted*

to meet Olivia's mother, but I figured if it ever had to be done, it would be in circumstances much better than these. "Shit."

"Any word from Nash yet?"

"No, but he should be—"

"Coming in the door right now," Nash says as he pushes the office door wider and steps inside. "I see you got the princess back in one piece."

I grit my teeth and ignore his comment. I thought we'd come to a sort of agreement to be civil, but it looks like that didn't last very long. I wonder to myself when it was, exactly, that my brother became such a douche. "Did you get Marissa to her dad's all right?"

"Yeah. But let me tell you, that is gonna be one messed-up female."

"Why? What happened?"

"I left her in the backseat until I got her to her dad's place. She didn't say much on the ride. She might've passed out or something. I don't know, but when I untied her and took her blindfold off and she saw me, I think it pushed her over the edge, man. She just started crying and threw her arms around my neck. I felt kinda bad for her. I guess once she recovers from being scared shitless, she'll be cursing the day she ever met you."

I clench my fingers into tight fists, but again, I ignore him.

"Was her father there? Did he say anything?"

"Yes, but I didn't give him a chance to say anything. I helped her to the door and was gonna see her on up to her bedroom, but he came down the steps, so I just left."

"Neither one of them said *anything*?"

"As I was walking out the door, I heard him ask her what the hell was going on, but other than that, I don't know. I shut the door and left."

"Well, I guess that's one way to do it." I should've known better than to expect any amount of tact and sensitivity from such a jackass.

"As much fun as it is to sit around and wait for you two to go at it, I need some sleep," Gavin says, getting to his feet and stretching, moving his shoulders in a circle.

"I think we could all use a little shut-eye."

"I'm not sleeping on the couch, so I guess I'll be borrowing your car again to go to the condo," Nash says.

"That's fine. Take your time, make yourself at home." I actually prefer it. Anything to get him and his attitude out of my hair. When he's like this, I get the feeling the guy is nothing but trouble.

"Thanks, *bro*." The sarcasm is unmistakable. I don't know what happened in the last few hours to get his dick all bent out of shape, but something sure did.

"I'll be back to go over the schedule and work for a while before we open," Gavin says before he opens the door leading back into the apartment.

"Cool. Get some rest, man. And thanks again." Gavin nods, and I turn grudgingly to my brother. "You, too, Nash."

Much to my surprise, he doesn't make any pissy comments; he just nods as well.

Poor bastard's probably bipolar or some shit like that. He's moodier than a damn woman!

I follow them out to lock up behind them. When I hear the sounds of the BMW fade as Nash drives off, I wander back to the bedroom. I stand in the doorway to watch Olivia. Seeing her relaxed in sleep, so peaceful and so *alive*, I feel myself start to calm. Within a few minutes, I become more and more aware of the effects of the last twelve hours. My muscles ache, a combination of tension and beating the shit out of a couple people. My head hurts, most likely from head-butting anonymous henchman number three. And the kisses from the two bullets I wasn't quite able to dodge are starting to sting, especially the one on my ribs.

Olivia whimpers in her sleep, causing a stab of guilt to prick my heart. It also causes me to feel something else, something that I don't really know what to do with and I'm not sure is entirely welcome. It feels an awful lot like a weakness, a weakness for her. And I don't want anything or anyone to be my weakness. Weakness makes you vulnerable, leaves you open to pain and loss. I've had enough of that to last a lifetime. No, I'm going to keep seeing Olivia, but I'll be keeping her at a safe distance.

I turn and make my way to the bathroom. I cut on the shower to as hot a temperature as I can stand then strip and step inside. I let the spray pound down on my face and chest, and then, many minutes later, I turn to let it beat down on my shoulders. Going through my head are all the ways that I can avoid getting too attached to Olivia.

I more feel her presence than hear her. It's like one minute she's in my head, and the next I open my eyes and she's standing in front of me. Naked. Sleepy. Sexy.

I start to speak, but she puts her finger over my mouth. She rubs my bottom lip almost absently. I flick my tongue out to touch her fingertip and her mouth falls open a tiny bit. Her eyes are on mine as she strokes the tip of my tongue. When I bite down, her eyes widen. I don't bite hard. Just enough that she can feel it, hopefully feel it all the way down to that sweet spot between her legs. And by the look in those eyes, I'd say that's exactly where she felt it.

Even over the noise of the shower, I hear her gasp. I know that she wants to be the one in control, but I will always be the one to push her. And she will always love it, crave it.

I let her finger go and she trails it down my chin and neck, then over to my left shoulder. Her eyebrows pull together into a frown when she traces the tender, skinned place where the first bullet grazed me. She leans in close and kisses it ever so sweetly.

She straightens and I watch her eyes roam my chest. When she sees where the second bullet nicked me on my side, she frowns up at me. "You were shot twice. Coming for me."

I shrug. "It's not like I was shot through the heart." Olivia closes her eyes for a second. When she opens them, I see the terror in them, the fear the words caused. I feel the urge to remove the fear, to replace it with something . . . happier. "You're not to blame. And you don't give love a bad name."

I watch her face as understanding dawns. I took a chance that she'd know the Bon Jovi song. And she does. During the sex-marathon weekend at her dad's place, she once mentioned, as we were lying in bed catching our breath, that her father loves classic rock. Said she grew up listening to it and had always liked it. Just one more thing I love about her.

"I'm glad that song doesn't apply to me." The corners of her mouth tilt up. Her mood is already lightening with the easy banter.

"Oh, no. If there were a song that applied to you, it would be 'Little Red Corvette.' "

"I'm nothing like that!"

"*You* don't think so, but I do. I see it. I see the fiery, racy, wild side of you that you try to ignore, try to hide. It's my mission in life to get you to take that thing out for a spin."

"Your mission in life, huh?"

"Yep." I reach out to trace her luscious bottom lip. As we fall quiet, I can see the weight fall back down on her shoulders. Suddenly, she looks exhausted again. "Here," I say, moving around behind her, where her back is to my chest and the spray of the shower is cascading down the front of her body. "Let me make you feel better."

She doesn't argue.

TWENTY-SEVEN

Olivia

Some sort of bell pulls me from a pleasantly oblivious state of rest. When I open my eyes, I'm greeted with the sight of Cash's naked body rising from the bed and walking across to the bathroom to grab his jeans from the floor and pull them on. When he comes back through the bedroom to head for the door, he sees me watching him. He grins. "See anything you like?"

I smile in return and waggle my eyebrows at him. He detours back to the bed. Throwing off the covers, Cash bends to drag one hand up my thigh while he pulls one of my nipples into his mouth. I catch my breath, instantly ready for him. He stops when his fingers are painfully close to where I most want him to touch me. He raises his head and gives me his wickedest, most promise-filled grin. "You think on that until I get back." He gives my lips a quick peck and jogs off toward the garage door.

I'm lying in bed, smiling like the Cheshire cat, when I hear Ginger.

"Is she here?"

"Yes. Would you like to speak to her?" I hear Cash respond.

"Of course. I didn't drive all the way down here to ask a simple question. Unless you want to make it worth my while." I grin and shake my head. I can almost see the smile she's wearing as she sharpens her cougar claws on Cash's chest. Before Cash, who is no doubt speechless, can respond, she continues. "Where is that disappearing wench? She scared the shit out of me!"

I look at the clock. No wonder she's upset. It's nearly seven p.m. I must've slept longer than I thought.

I pull the covers up tighter around me and sit up just as Ginger is coming into the bedroom. "There you are," she says, flinging her arms. "And just as I suspected. I've been worrying my ass off and you've been having multiple orgasms at the end of a Greek god's penis. Figures."

"I'm sorry, Ginger. I didn't mean to worry you. It's that stupid phone I'm using. I can't wait to get mine back."

"That's a likely story. But hell, I'd lie, too, if this were waiting for me back here." With a smile, she perches on the edge of the bed beside me. "No worries. I'm just happy to see your henhouse being taken care of by such a fabulous cock." She leans in and whispers to me, "And it is a fabulous cock, am I right?" I say nothing, simply grin. She leans back and clears her throat. "I expected nothing less. God doesn't mess something like *that* up," she says, hiking her thumb back toward Cash, who is hovering in the doorway, clearly already bored with Ginger's presence.

"No, He didn't mess up *anything* on that!" I gloat.

"You're a saucy bitch to tease me this way. Where's the other one? They're twins. He ought to be just as perfect. Only a little less . . . attached."

Ginger grins at me, and I roll my eyes just as I hear the door open. I see Cash turn toward the garage, and then I hear another voice.

"I hope it's a bad time," Nash says in his gruff way. He steps into the doorway and looks in at me. "Damn, you lucked up. I love a girl that doesn't mind company."

If the sting in my cheeks is any indication, my face is cherry red at his insinuation. Before anyone can respond, Ginger turns to me, her eyes wide. "Sweet mother of sex, they're triplets!"

Ginger looks back toward Nash and my eyes meet Cash's. I'm fine until he winks. Then I lose it. We both burst into laughter.

"What?" Ginger asks, turning to look back at me. She narrows her eyes at me and gasps. "You've been hiding them from me *on purpose*! You naughty, naughty little vixen!" She pauses for only a second before she throws her arms around my neck. "Never in all my wildest dreams did I take you for a foursome. With triplets, no less!" She leans back and grins at me. "You've officially earned your claws. Not the cougar kind, of course. You're far too young for that. But you get honorary claws just for being the only hen in a whole house full of cocks. I'm so proud," she says melodramatically, covering her mouth with her hands. I know she's just teasing when she winks at me over her polished nails.

"God, you're incorrigible."

She drops her hands and kills the drama. "I know. But that's why you love me." She stands and tugs at the hem of her short skirt. "Well, boys, I'd have been happy to join this little party, but I'm thinking it's already a bit crowded. I wouldn't want to overwhelm anyone with my fabulousness. Maybe next time." With her typical cocky strut, Ginger makes her way from the room, reaching behind her to slap Nash on the butt as she passes. I see her turn and give him a cheeky wink as she goes.

"Who the hell was that?" Nash asks.

"You don't want to know," Cash replies.

"I heard that," Ginger chimes in from the garage, her voice echoing back to us. I hear her mumble something else for a few seconds before another voice sounds.

"Hello?"

Marissa.

Oh shit!

I hear a light knock, like she rapped on the door frame with her knuckles. I look to Cash, and he sighs heavily through thinned lips. "Dammit!" I hear him mutter. "Couldn't you people have called?" he says testily.

"I'm sorry," I hear Marissa say. "I was looking for . . . him." I imagine her indicating Nash. He's the only *him* in the room other than Cash.

"Fine," Cash says abruptly. "You found him. Why don't you two take the office? You can have some privacy." I see him trying to push Nash out of the way and shut the door, but not before Marissa gets into the apartment far enough to see into the bedroom. Into where I'm still lying naked in the bed, covered only in a rumpled sheet.

She looks in, and I see a frown flicker across her forehead before she rushes past Cash toward me. She launches herself at the bed, throwing her arms around my neck. I'm stunned, of course, and left wondering what's going on while I try to keep myself covered. The room is far too full for my current state of undress.

"I'm so glad you're okay," she murmurs against my neck. I feel her body shake. It takes me a minute to realize she's silently sobbing.

"Marissa, what's wrong?" I ask this more out of shock than any real concern. My cousin has been a royal bitch since birth, and any love between us died about six months thereafter.

She leans away and looks back at me with huge, watery blue eyes. The most puzzling thing is that they seem to be *sincere* huge, watery blue eyes.

"I was so afraid for you. I heard them talking about killing you. Both of us. *All* of us," she says, turning to look back at the twins, standing quietly in the doorway. "I've never been so scared in all my life. And all I could think about was sending you to that damned art exhibition wearing that stupid dress."

I'm dumbstruck. And completely suspicious. I'm adult enough to admit it. This girl, whom I've often fantasized about scalping or setting on fire or dyeing purple, suddenly gets *nice*? Um, I don't think so.

"I know you probably think I'm crazy. Or making it up. But I swear to you, Liv, you were all I could think about." Her lip starts to tremble and her eyes fill with more tears. "You've always been good to me, always been such a sweet person, and I've always treated you like nothing. And I'm so sorry. All my life, I've been surrounded by people just like me. People who probably couldn't care less if I disappeared. And that includes Daddy. What I needed most was to be surrounded by people just like you." She pauses and swallows hard, tears streaming down her face. "I don't want to be that person anymore, Liv. Can you ever forgive me?"

Holy cousin of brain damage! Marissa's had a stroke.

That's the only plausible explanation. The. Only. One. People like her don't suffer crises of conscience. People like her don't have changes of heart. People like her don't have hearts, *period*.

But as I look into her eyes, I'm struck again by how sincere she seems. She appears to be genuinely contrite, genuinely distressed about this.

"It wasn't that big a deal, Marissa. Don't stress over it. I think you just need to go back home and get some rest."

"No, I don't. I don't need rest. I need to know you forgive me. And then I need to talk to him," she says, looking back over her shoulder at Nash. I don't think she's even spared Cash a glance since she walked in.

I wonder what she thinks, what she knows.

"Where is my daughter?"

My heart sinks when I hear that voice. I glance at Cash. Even from across the room, I see him stiffen.

My first inclination is to hide under the covers. That, of course, is not an option. The best I can do is sit up nice and straight and take it like a woman, a woman who is old enough to make her own decisions.

Mom stops in the bedroom doorway and stares at both Cash and Nash. It's a withering glare that would make my balls shrivel. If I had any, that is. I guess I'm having sympathy ball shriveling. It's not a good feeling.

Nash steps slightly to the side, giving her a wide berth as she enters the room. Cash doesn't move at all, except to extend his hand.

"I'm Cash Davenport. You must be Olivia's mother."

"And why must I be? I'm sure she's told you nothing about me. If she had, you'd know better than to pull a stunt like this with my daughter."

"It's enough that I know your daughter. It speaks highly of you that you gave birth to and helped raise someone like her."

"If you think so much of my daughter, why is she in this position?"

"She's in this position because she's a good person who wanted to help someone. Who wanted to help me. She's *here* because I'm trying to keep her safe."

"Well, you've done a bang-up job so far," my mother snaps, pushing past him and making her way to me. I see Cash's jaw clench before my chin is in my mother's palm, my face being examined. "Are you hurt?"

"No, Mom. I'm fine. Cash and Gavin found me and took care of everything."

"Cash, Gavin, Gabe. Where do you meet this trash? I thought getting out of Salt Springs would be good for you, but you might just be the kind of girl that falls for this . . . type no matter where you live."

"Mom, I didn't—"

"I see that Olivia's mother made it." I peek around my mother. Gavin has appeared in the bedroom doorway as well.

Next time I'm having an impromptu toga party so I can be the only appropriately dressed person in the room.

"And you! You're the one who got her in this mess in the first place. If you'd simply driven her to school like she'd asked you to do . . ."

Gavin hangs his head at that, mainly because she's right.

"You can't blame him for that, Mom. He thought he was doing the right thing. Which he obviously was, since that's where I was attacked."

Mom turns her icy eyes back on me. "Honestly, have you no shame? No pride? No sense of self-worth? Letting people like this tell you what to do, get you into trouble? Whoring around with men like this?"

"That's enough!" Cash booms from behind her. "She may be your daughter, but that doesn't give you the right to talk to her like that."

"Oh yes, it does. The only person out of line here is *you*. I assume you're the one she's shacked up with? You're the one defiling my daughter on a regular basis? Not enough respect for her to marry her. You just use her like some cheap dime-store floozy."

"I'm not using her. And I—"

My mother waves her hand imperiously and cuts Cash off. "I'm not interested in your excuses. I'm here to collect my daughter and get her out of your life. I'll ask that you kindly stay out of ours." She turns back to me and commands, "Now get dressed. You're coming home with me."

"No, I'm not, Mom. I'm staying here. I'm a grown woman. You can't keep treating me this way."

"As long as you keep acting this way, I'll keep treating you this way."

"Acting what way? So I've made some mistakes, made some bad judgments. Is that so terrible? Is that so abnormal? You made mistakes, and look at you. Do you think I'd make the same decisions you've made if it meant I'd turn out cold and miserable and alone?"

"I'm none of those things, Olivia."

"You are, you just don't know it. You picked the perfect man who gave you the perfect house and the perfect car and the perfect life, but you're miserable. You loved Daddy, but you somehow got it in your head that he wasn't good enough, that life on a farm wasn't good enough. Well, I'm not you, Mom. I'd rather have a life full of love and happiness than all the money in the world."

"And that would be fine with me, but if you think someone like this," she says, jacking her thumb back over her shoulder at Cash, "is the man who can give you anything but heartache, think again."

"Mom, he risked his life to save me."

"He's the one who put you in danger."

"No, I put myself in danger. I knew the risk, but I wanted to help."

"What on earth could be so important that you'd do something so foolish, Olivia?"

"Someone's life, Mother."

"Someone you don't even know. Am I right?"

I pause. "Yes, but—"

"But nothing. That was yet another decision that shows you are incapable of taking care of yourself. That's why I'm going to do it."

"I did it for love, Mom. I did it for Cash. Because I love him. It was important to him, therefore it was important to me. Why can't you understand that?"

"Oh, I understand that just fine. It simply means you've picked another doozy who will get you into a world of hurt and then leave you when you're no longer a fun diversion. He's worthless just like—"

"Mother, stop it!" I shout. She takes a step back as if I'd physically slapped her. "Not all guys who look a certain way or dress a certain way or act a certain way are the same. You've tried all my life to drive me toward the kind of guy *you* wanted me to be with. You made me feel as though there were something wrong with me for liking anyone who rode a motorcycle or drove a muscle car or played in a band. But there was never anything wrong with them, Mom. They just weren't for me. I wouldn't have wanted to end up with any of them. Not now. But you don't see that. You don't see that now and you didn't see that then. You could never be like a normal mother, one who holds her daughter when she cries and tells her that one day she'll find Mr. Right, that one day love will be worth it. That was just beyond you. You had to do your best, at every possible opportunity, to convince me that the *only* way I'd ever be happy would be with a guy like Lyle, one who is so focused on his job and his money that he doesn't have time for love. But, Mom, if falling in love means risking getting hurt, then I'm okay with that. Because finally, for once, I've found someone worth the risk. I wouldn't have missed out on Cash for the world, Mom. Did it ever occur to you that it took all those heartbreaks, all those tears, all those failed attempts to be able to recognize something real when I found it? Can't you just be happy for me and leave us in peace?"

Absolute silence falls across the room. My mother is watching me like I skinned her pet rabbit to wear as a hat. Marissa is frowning. Nash looks bored. Gavin is smiling. And Cash looks . . . like he's walking toward me.

His eyes are locked on mine as he approaches. He steps right in front of my mother and stops. He watches me for a few seconds before his lips curve into a satisfied smile. It gets wider as he leans down to me. I think he might laugh, but he sobers as he reaches out to cup my face in his hands.

And then he kisses me. Not just a small kiss, either. A good kiss. A really good kiss. A kiss that other people should not be witnessing, especially when I'm wearing a sheet and nothing else.

"I love it when you get fiery," he says after he pulls his lips away. His eyes are sparkling chips of onyx as they search mine. Gently, he rubs his thumbs over my cheekbones and smiles again. It shines down onto my face like the sun, warm and healing. Slowly, deliberately, he reaches down to take my free hand and lace his fingers with mine, and then he straightens and turns toward my mother. "She's staying here, ma'am. You're always welcome to visit her because you're her mother, but right now, I think it'd be best if you left. I'll take good care of her. You've got my word. That might not mean much to you, but it means a hell of a lot to me. And so does your daughter."

Mom looks from Cash to me and back again before she turns and pins everyone in the room with her proud, cold stare. With a tight smile, she speaks to me as she backs toward the door. "Fine. If this is how you want it, Olivia, go right ahead and ruin your life. Just don't come crying to me when it all falls apart."

"I love you, Mom, but I stopped running to you years ago. It never me did any good."

She nods once, an arrogant dip of her head, before she turns and walks slowly from the room, leaving nothing in her wake but expensive perfume, frigid air, and relief.

No one says anything for a few minutes, not until Gavin breaks the tense silence. "Damn, that woman is one mighty bitch. I think my balls just now dropped back down."

We all look at each other and then everyone bursts into laughter, Marissa included. I find myself watching her most of all. She can't seem to keep her eyes off Nash. I can't help but wonder if she's really a changed person, if this new Marissa will hang around for long or if the wicked witch will chase her off with her evil broom of doom and gloom. Only time will tell, but I hope *this girl* is here to stay.

The ring of a cell phone breaks into the moment. It's coming from Cash's dresser. He releases my hand to grab it. I watch him pick up his personal cell phone, not one of the burners, and look at the screen. His brow is wrinkled as he answers it. I'm immediately uneasy when he walks out of the bedroom. I hear the door to the office close behind him. My stomach curls into a tight knot of dread.

For just a moment, I was able to forget what danger we're still in.

TWENTY-EIGHT

Cash

When I answered and heard the words, "Did you place the ad?" I knew it was Dad's second line of defense. Assuming, of course, that Nash was the first. It's entirely possible, however, that this one could be *even more* helpful. I can only hope so.

After I close the office door behind me, I respond. "Yes, I placed the ad."

"Get another phone. Get on the road by nine tonight. Call this number at six minutes after. I'll give further instructions."

The line goes dead, leaving me aggravated. I would've at least liked to ask a couple questions. Of course, when I think about it, it's probably not smart to say much of anything over my personal phone. Unfortunately, that does nothing to soothe my irritation.

My mind goes straight into planning mode, into strategizing.

The thing I'm most focused on, however, is not protecting myself; it's what to do with Olivia while I'm gone. How best to keep her safe.

Gavin's a great guy and he did his best, but now I'm leery of leaving her in anyone else's care. I think of my options and realize that aside from taking her with me, which I refuse to do because it could be very dangerous, the place she would likely be safest is behind the bar here at Dual. In front of hundreds of witnesses. Never alone.

Now breaking this to Olivia without sounding like an insensitive ass is the hard part. I mean, how does one approach that?

Your life has been turned completely upside down because of me and my family, your apartment was ransacked, you were kidnapped and drugged, you had a run-in with both your cold bitch cousin and your ice queen mother, but could you please work a shift at my club tonight?

Yeah, that's not gonna happen.

Marching back into the bedroom, I do what I should've done when the doorbell first rang.

"All right, everybody, out! I need to talk to Olivia, and you need to give her some privacy to get dressed."

No one argues, of course. In fact, Gavin looks a little sheepish that he's been so rude. It was really thoughtless on *all* our parts to keep her in this position. Leave it to Olivia to be so cool, so composed while surrounded by people and having tough conversations, all while she's wrapped in bedclothes. Underneath all that lush beauty, she's got a backbone of steel. I hope, after today, she comes to realize that.

"Thank you for that," she says when Gavin closes the door behind the exiting trio.

"I'm sorry for not doing it sooner."

"Well, it's not like there was a good time. It was like a circus in here! All we lacked was a bearded lady and a sword swallower, although Ginger might be able to swallow something nearly that big."

She giggles and the sound makes me want to hug her. I don't know why really, but it does.

"Well, as the ringleader of this most recent circus surrounding your life, I apologize for failing you."

A soft look falls down over Olivia's features. Her green eyes are piercing, like a sweet hurt, as they watch me. Her gaze never leaving mine, she lets the cover fall from her breasts and she slides off the edge of the bed, walking slowly toward me, naked as the day she was born. Only a thousand times more beautiful.

She stops when the tips of her nipples are brushing my chest. "You haven't failed me. You've breathed so much life into my existence. Don't ever be sorry for that."

"But I—"

"Shhh," she says, placing a finger over my mouth. She's fond of doing that. "Don't. Please."

I nod and work to control my body's reaction to her close proximity. I need to learn to tolerate being around her, learn to think of things other than tearing off her clothes with my teeth and sinking into her like a soft, wet bed of rose petals.

I clear my throat and focus on the reason I came to her to begin with. "The call I got a few minutes ago . . ."

Her expression turns serious, concerned. "Yeah. What was that all about?"

"It was about the second ad I placed. I need to meet with him tonight. But the thing is, I'm not comfortable leaving you. At all, really, but I know it's not a good idea to take you with me, so I don't have much choice."

"Don't worry about me," she says sweetly. "I'll be fine."

"Of course I'll worry about you. But I think I've figured out a way to ensure your safety. If you're agreeable to it, that is."

"What is it?"

She looks suspicious, which I think is kind of funny.

"It doesn't involve you being locked in a room anywhere, if that's what you're thinking." The look on her face tells me that's *exactly* what she was thinking. "In fact, this is something you've done before."

"Which is . . ." she prompts when I don't finish.

"How about working a shift tonight? I think behind a bar with hundreds of people watching you is just about the safest place I could keep you."

"That's fine. Why didn't you just say so? You had me worried."

"Because I don't want you to think I'm an insensitive ass-hole. You've had a shitty day. A *really* shitty day and—"

"Not all of it's been shitty," she says, looking up at me from beneath her thick lashes. Takes me right back to having to work to think of things *other than* her riding me like a prize stallion.

"Well, bad enough. Let's just put it that way. Anyway, asking you to work sounds like something a selfish bastard would do, and I don't want you to think—"

"You're not a selfish bastard. Didn't you hear a word I said to my mother?"

"Yes, but—"

"No *but*s. Cash, I love you."

Like the dumbass that I am, a fact that I blame solely on my possession of testicles, I freeze. I say nothing. I don't tell her all the things I'm feeling. I don't say all the things that need saying. I just look at her. Like an asshole.

I can see the disappointment on her face, and it kills me to watch her fight through it. But she does. She comes out on the other side, smiling and swinging, even though her heart probably feels like neither.

"Besides, I think work will be good for me. Keep my mind occupied."

"Are you sure?"

"I'm positive," she says agreeably, heartache oozing through the pleasant exterior of her expression. "I'm gonna get a shower. A real one this time," she teases, trying her damnedest to project lightheartedness. She stretches up on her toes and brushes her lips across mine. "Thank Gavin for bringing my bag."

"Did he bring your stuff?"

"He must have. I just noticed it sitting in the corner a minute ago."

"Hmmm. Okay, I'll tell him."

"Thanks," she says with a smile before she moves around

me and heads for the bathroom. Meanwhile I'm left standing in the same spot, watching her go, feeling like a steaming pile of crap.

"You're not going without me," Nash barks adamantly.

"Or me," Gavin chimes in.

"The hell I'm not! Somebody has to stay here and keep an eye on Olivia. And it can't be me."

"Then it's gonna have to be Gavin, because I'm not staying here to be grilled by some female Johnnie Cochran. I'm not answering questions Marissa should be asking *you*," Nash gripes.

It wasn't easy to talk Marissa into coming back to the club at a later time. I promised she could talk to Nash all night if she wanted to, but that now just wasn't a good time. She left, albeit grudgingly. I have no doubt she'll be back the instant the club opens. Obviously Nash thinks the same thing. Seems like he's still a pretty perceptive guy. Having only just met her, he was able to tell that Marissa's as tenacious as a pit bull. That's probably one of the reasons she's such a good attorney.

For a few seconds, I consider letting him come along. With the exception of a couple of disastrous worst-case scenarios (like this mystery guy putting a bullet in *both* our heads), it's probably a good idea for him to come no matter how I slice it. Having some backup is never a bad thing.

"Fine. Nash and I will go. Gavin, you stay here and watch out for Olivia." I can tell he doesn't like it, but he'll do it. He nods curtly. "Man, you know I don't trust anyone else to protect her. And knowing what you've already done for her . . ."

That softens him up a little. All us men have our egos, after all. "I know, mate. I'll keep her safe."

"I hope you do a better job of it this time than last," Nash injects snidely. Gavin gives him a smile, but it's a chilly smile. Nash doesn't know him well enough to know he's treading on dangerous ground. Gavin can give a person that same smile right as he puts a gun to their head. My father used to talk about his demeanor. "Cold as ice," he'd say of Gavin. But in every other way, I find him to be a nice guy. He's just a nice guy who would kill you if you crossed him or his friends or family. That's all.

"My advice, Nash," I say, looking at him seriously. He raises his eyebrows in question. "Don't piss him off. You really don't want to do that."

He nods casually as he glances sideways at the still-smiling Gavin.

"All right, so that's the plan. Nash and I will go to the meet, you stay here with Olivia. I'll get back as soon as I can."

"I've got it covered."

Nash and I decide to drive separately, just in case. It's impossible to anticipate everything, but I can't help but be a little suspicious of . . . well, everyone, really. I'm trying to be realistic about the likelihood of the person I'm about to meet being a criminal. And criminals are very unpredictable. And if this one decides to pull something, having a second means of escape is wise.

Before we left, I punched the number of the guy who called into one of the burner phones I'd bought. I'm in the car so I can hear him clearly. Nash is following on my bike.

When we've been on the road for a couple of minutes, I dial the number.

He answers on the first ring. "Meet me at the Ronin Shipping Company's boatyard in twenty minutes." He hangs up. Again.

Damn, that irks the shit out of me.

I grit my teeth and suck it up, though. I don't have much choice. I try to keep one eye on the road as I input the information into the car's navigation. It reroutes me back toward the club and beyond, so I find the first place I can to do a U-turn. Nash is right on my heels.

Just under twenty minutes later, I'm pulling up to the gated entrance of what looks like a huge cemetery for commercial boats. I can see their enormous shapes like black ghosts in the fog.

I stare at the closed gate and tall perimeter fence, wondering how the hell we're supposed to get inside. Before I can get out to talk to Nash, however, the gate clanks just before it slides slowly to the left.

I roll my window down. On high alert, senses reaching out for everything from sound to movement, I edge the car into the crowded lot. The fog only adds to the ominous feeling of the meet. My headlights cut through it, but still give me visibility for only a few feet in front of me. Add to that the claustrophobic sensation created by the looming ships on either side and it's downright creepy.

I hit the brakes when my lights shine on a person standing in the middle of the road. He fits in perfectly with the overall setting of the night. He's wearing an old, black rain slicker and a wharf hat, also in faded black. All he lacks is a hook for a hand. Or an army of the dead. Either way . . .

I stop and wait to see what he's going to do. He waves one hand, which is thankfully a hand and not a shiny piece of curved metal, and motions me forward. I follow him. Behind me, I see the single headlight of the motorcycle. Nash is following closely.

Smart.

The cloaked figure leads us to a small shacklike structure. Maybe a place where someone would sit and communicate with crane operators or something like that. The guy turns to me and waves his hand for me to come inside. I put the car in park and cut the engine. I climb out from behind the wheel, my muscles bunched and ready to kick some ass if need be.

Nash comes up to my left. I glance at him. He looks serious and deadly. If I didn't know him, I might think he's intimidating. Well, no, I wouldn't. It takes a lot to intimidate me. But I can see where other people might find him disconcerting. It makes me wonder again what's happened to him that's made him this way. He's so different from the kid I used to know.

I guess we both are.

We approach the shack's door. The guy walks inside and

sits in the chair behind a console covered in buttons and levers. He pulls off his hat and looks right at Nash.

I recognize him instantly—ruddy complexion, puffy face, bushy brown hair, and flat blue eyes. I saw him earlier today.

Like the strike of a snake, Nash has a gun in this guy's face. And I don't blame him one bit for putting it there. But I *have to know* what the hell is going on before I let Nash put a bullet in this man's skull. I have to know why Dad would bring Duffy into this as someone to help.

I hear the soft click of the safety and realize Nash is close to losing it. "Nash, no! We need to talk to him first."

"We don't need anything from this guy but blood. Lots and lots of blood." His voice is eerily calm.

"We need to know what he has that Dad thinks we need, that he thinks we can use."

For the first time, Duffy, who doesn't seem the least bit bothered by the gun in his face, speaks. "I was a friend of your father's." His Russian accent is so light, it's barely discernible. But still, I can tell it's there. He must've been in the States for quite a while now.

"Then you should die for being a traitor as well as a murderer."

"Maybe for being a murderer, but never for being a traitor. I was a friend to both your parents. A loyal friend. I knew how much Greg wanted to get out. And not for his sake. For yours. And Lizzie's."

Hearing him speak my mother's name sets my teeth on edge. It's like hearing the devil himself whisper it.

"Well, you certainly proved that when you rigged the boat with explosives and then pulled the trigger, didn't you?"

"You weren't supposed to be there with the supplies that early. I had no way of knowing she'd be on that boat."

"Maybe you shouldn't have blown it up to begin with. I think that's something more in line with what a friend would do," Nash growls.

"Your father knew I had to do it, to keep up appearances. He knew they'd be suspicious of everyone after the books disappeared."

"The books? It was *you* that got him the books?"

Duffy nods, and I feel a little sick to my stomach. The more I learn about my family, about my father and his dealings, the more I want out of it all, away from it all. Away from him. And probably Nash, too.

"Ask yourself this: If your father didn't really trust me, would he have had me, of all people, help you?"

He has a good point, but I still don't trust a word he says. To be honest, I'm having a hard time wrapping my head around all this shit. There are too few people to trust and far too many criminals. There are too few answers and far too many lies. Far, far, far too many lies.

"Honestly, I really don't know. The only person I trust right now is me. So I think what you'd better do is tell us how you can help, then get the hell out of here. Because I can guarantee you, the next time either of us sees you, we'll be seeing your brains, too. All over the ground."

Duffy nods. "Fair enough." His docile manner actually does

seem like the actions of someone who's had to live with guilt for a lot of years. Just like Nash's irrational, half-cocked behavior seems like the actions of someone who's had to live with criminals for a lot of years. Criminals and an insatiable lust for revenge.

"Well then, why are you here?"

"I'm going to blackmail Anatoli, Slava's right-hand man, into getting me the books back. He's the only one Slava really trusts."

"And you think whatever you have on him is enough to get him to do this?"

"Yes, I do. It's enough to get me killed, too. But I owe your father. He could've pointed the guilty finger at me, could've told them that I'm the one who took the books, but he didn't. And, to repay him, I killed his wife. I owe him this, to take this chance."

"I'd say you do, you lousy bastard," Nash spits.

"But once I get you the books, you have to be prepared to move quickly. I can give you a little more help with that by providing you with some important lists that will help tie your case together, but the rest is up to you. If you blow this chance, there's nothing I can do to help you but attend your funeral."

"You have to know there's not a snowball's chance in hell that we'd take your word for it, right?"

Duffy nods once. "Go see your father. Just be careful what you say. They have people everywhere. As you've been finding out."

He's right. I have. The hard way.

"Then what?"

"Then I'll be in touch when I have the books and the lists. After that, you'll never hear from me again."

"I can only hope that means what I think it means," Nash sneers.

"It means I'll be disappearing one way or the other. This country won't be safe for me anymore. My family . . ."

"Oh, cry me a river. Because of you, this is all the family I have left," Nash shouts angrily.

"Then we'll be even. I won't owe your family anything else."

"You'll always—"

"Nash," I say to cut him off. No sense making threats until we talk to Dad. If we can use this guy and it keeps Olivia safe, I have to leave the possibility open, no matter how distasteful it is. She's worth it. "We need to talk to Dad."

I look at him, hoping he sees what I mean by my stare. When he takes a deep breath and clenches his teeth, I see that he does. He knows this is how it has to be if he's going to get his revenge.

"And you should know that I didn't know it was your girlfriend they sent me after. I knew I was picking up a girl named Olivia Townsend and she was being used to get some books before being . . . disposed of. I didn't know it was you until I saw you at the warehouse."

Now I can sympathize with Nash a little more. I see red. Or black maybe. All I can think of is that this guy had come for Olivia. The fact that he wasn't the one who took her, that he took Marissa instead, makes no difference. The fact of the matter is that he intended to kidnap and then kill Olivia.

"Calm down, right, brother? Wait until we talk to Dad, right, brother?" There's smug sarcasm in Nash's voice. I should've known he'd enjoy this. But at the moment, I couldn't care less. I'm struggling with every ounce of self-control that I possess *not* to beat this man to death with my fists, to see his blood spraying all over his face and dripping down his shirt as I pound and pound and pound on him, not stopping until I feel better, until I'm no longer picturing him holding a gun to Olivia's head.

I turn and walk out of the shack. I need air. Lots of air and lots of space. Being so close to the man who not only killed my mother but was contemplating doing the same thing to Olivia is just too much for me to bear without ripping someone's throat out. I'm smart enough to know when my control is slipping, though. So getting out is my only option. I'll leave Nash to follow me when he's done. And at this point, if he kills the guy after I leave, then so be it. We'll find another way.

I hope.

TWENTY-NINE

Olivia

I bet I've looked at the office door ten thousand times, hoping each time to see Cash's face there. I'm on pins and needles. It's like a sharp knife to the gut every time I think of him not returning my confession of love. But I love him. I'm *in* love with him. I can't imagine living the rest of my life knowing he died to save me. If I never get to be with him, never get to live the dream with him, never get his whole heart, it would never change the fact that I love him more than I've ever loved anyone or anything. And just the thought of him leaving this earth, this life because of me is unbearable. Even if I can't have him, just knowing he's alive . . . and healthy . . . and safe . . . would be enough.

Just knowing he's out there . . . somewhere . . .

For the thousandth time, I feel the burn of tears at the backs of my eyes.

Please God, please God, please God.

That mantra has gone through my head almost continually. I don't know how in the world I've made a single drink tonight. I must have a pretty freakin' awesome autopilot. As long as it's not dressing me, that is.

Once more, I glance at the door. As my eyes are drifting away, rife with disappointment, they pass Marco. He smiles. It's not a flirtatious smile or a particularly happy smile. It's more a smile of sympathy. I wonder what he's thinking, what he knows.

I'm not sure why I even care anymore. If things don't work out with Cash and me, I won't be working here any longer, anyway, so what's the big deal?

You're an idiot. That's the big deal.

True. Very true.

I see the house lights dim. That's how I know a slow song is coming up in the rotation. That's just what I need right now—a sappy love song to finish ripping my heart out.

I recognize the Saigon Kick song after the first few bars. My father taught me well.

As I suspected, it feels like a knife to the chest. The worry over Cash coupled with the lyrics is enough to take my breath. Literally. For a few seconds I feel like I can't breathe.

But then, suddenly, I can.

There, standing in the doorway of the office, is Cash. His eyes lock with mine and I feel them, really *feel* them all through my body. It's like standing naked in the middle of the night during a warm summer rain. He's everywhere. He's on my skin, under my skin, in my heart, in my soul.

I feel like I might burst with the desire to go to him. It takes every ounce of my willpower to stay put, to school my expression. To pretend. But I do it. Somehow, I do it.

Until he starts toward me.

And then I stop. Stop everything. Stop moving, stop breathing, stop thinking. All I can do is stare as Cash's long legs eat up the distance between us. Without a single word, he shoulders his way through the crush of people. When he reaches me, he steps up to the bar, reaches across it, and offers me his hand.

His eyes are still on mine and the rest of the world has disappeared. Suddenly it doesn't matter who's watching. Nothing matters but Cash. Nothing ever has. And nothing ever will again.

I slide my fingers into his and he tugs on my hand. I step onto the rail and put one knee on the bar. Cash releases my hand, reaches forward, and sweeps me off the slick countertop and into his arms.

I can feel his breath, coming hot and fast, fanning my cheeks. I can feel his need, wild and hungry, searing my soul. And, for just a second, I think I can feel his love, too. It burns me, but in a completely different way. Like a brand that says I'll always be his and he'll always be mine.

And then he drops his head and his lips cover mine. Vaguely, I hear shouts and hollers and clapping, but I don't care. I don't care who sees or who knows or how they feel about it. I care about the man carrying me. Always carrying me.

When Cash lifts his head, his mouth is curved into a mischievous smile.

"Have I told you that I love you?" he asks.

My heart does a triple somersault right inside my chest, one I feel is mirrored in my beaming smile.

"No. I'm pretty sure I would've remembered that."

Cash starts walking toward the side stairs, the ones that lead to the VIP room where I first met him. I don't care where he takes me, just as long as he doesn't let me go.

Ever.

"Well, it's your own fault. Every time I had a great opportunity to tell you, you beat me to the punch. And you know as well as I do that I'm not the kind of guy to let someone steal his thunder. I like my thunder big. And loud."

"Oh, I know you do," I tease. "And this time," I say, tipping my head back toward the cheering crowd, "you've got it. In spades."

"The funny thing is, the only thing I want is you. Just you. If it were up to me, I'd make the world disappear and it would be just us. Just you and me."

"I wish you were a magician."

"Well, I'm not a magician, but I do have a few tricks up my sleeve," he says with a wink.

"You do?"

"I do. Wanna see?"

"Of course."

Taking the stairs two at a time, at the top, Cash bends so I can open the VIP room door long enough for him to slip inside. It closes automatically behind us.

He carries me to the center of the room and sets me on my feet. I look around at the interior that signified the day my life would change forever. It doesn't look any different physically—black carpet, black walls, crazy lights, one whole wall of two-way mirrors that look like windows, and the bar that sits in front of them—but it feels like night and day.

As if someone—cough, Marco, cough—knew we were coming up here, the music cranks up and a song called "Lick It Up" comes on. I walk to the windows and peek down at the bar. Marco is smiling up at me. He salutes as though he can see me, and I laugh.

"I seem to remember some unfinished business up here. Does any of that ring a bell?"

"Why, I can't *imagine* what you could be referring to," I say with wide eyes and my most innocent Southern accent.

"I think I'm wearing too many clothes. And I think you need to take care of that. Now. Starting with this pesky shirt."

Cash holds out his arms, much like he did the first night I met him. I walk slowly toward him and reach around his waist, untucking his shirt, much like I did the first night I met him. My breasts brush his chest and his eyes set my body on fire, *exactly* like they did the first night I met him.

I tug his shirt over his head and toss it aside.

"Now the jeans," he commands. One brow shoots up and he adds, "On your knees."

Obediently, I drop to my knees in front of him. My eyes on his, I reach out and unbutton his jeans. I can feel his impressive hardness straining against the seams as my wrist grazes his zipper. I start to lower it, but he stops me with his words. "With your teeth."

A little thrill of excitement races through me, but I comply. Reaching around him, I plant both my hands on his firm, round butt and I lean in to nuzzle his jeans until I can get to the tiny golden pull on his zipper. I use my tongue to pick it up and grab it between my teeth, and I see Cash catch his breath. I smile as I tug the zipper open, freeing him.

Getting into his little game of torture, I squeeze his butt and pull him closer to my mouth as I run my tongue from the base of his thick shaft all the way to the tip. I hear him groan as I close my lips around the head. His fingers dive into my hair and contract, holding me to him for just one second.

"Pull them down," he croaks, his voice hoarse. I'm pleased with his level of excitement. Two can play this game.

I don't tell him what a pleasure it is to run my hands inside his waistband, to let my palms glide over his smooth, perfectly rounded cheeks, to let my fingertips coast down his powerful thighs. I don't tell him how flawless he is, that I've never known a more impeccably built man.

When I get to his ankles, he kicks off his shoes and steps out of his jeans. I rise slowly to stand, letting my eyes and my fingers trail over every hard inch of him as I do.

He leans forward to kiss me, but I dart quickly away, doing my best to strut to the bar.

If he wants to play, we'll play.

I push my shoes off my feet and turn to lean back against the bar before hoisting myself onto it. My eyes never leaving his, I rise to my feet, towering over him as I move my hips to the beat of the heavy bass. I know by the look on his face that he wants inside me. Right now. Right this minute. And very badly. But I won't let him. Not yet.

If he wants a stripper, I'll give him a stripper.

Slowly, I cross my arms over my chest, curling my fingers in the hem of my tank, and I drag it, inch by inch, up my body and slide it gently over my head. I shake my hair loose of the neck and throw the tiny swatch of black material at Cash. He catches it and, with a wicked grin, brings it to his face and inhales.

Letting the pleasure I feel in my soul ooze out, I smile at Cash as I unbutton and unzip my jeans, wiggling my hips as I push them down my legs. I see his eyes travel with them. I feel them like a touch—heated and urgent.

I step out of the material and, with a flick of my foot, kick them at Cash as well. He catches them and, just as he did with my tank, he brings them to his face and inhales. His eyes sparkle at me from over the top of them.

I slide first one bra strap then the other down my arms, revealing most of the tops of my breasts, but not the nipples. Coyly, I turn my back to him, peeking at him over my shoulder as I unhook the lacy band and pull it off. He grins and cocks one eyebrow at me. I wink and toss him my bra.

Again, he takes the cloth and buries his face in it, breathing in deeply. He closes his eyes as he does, like he's breathing in a part of me, a part of my soul.

I wait for him to open his eyes before I slide my hands down my sides and under the band of my panties. I can almost taste his anticipation. It's thick in the air. So I pause. And I smile. His perfect eyes are on mine and his perfect white teeth are biting into his perfect lower lip. He nods once and I see him reach down and palm his erection, sliding his fingers slowly up and down the length.

I feel an ache low in my stomach that assures me I'm as much a victim of this game as he is. But I can't stop now.

I ease my panties down just a fraction. Cash's eyes fall to my butt and I see him take a breath and hold it. I turn ever so slightly to the side and, as slowly as I can, I drag the material down my legs, bending sharply at the waist. I hear Cash make a noise that tells me he's very much enjoying what I'm doing, what he's seeing. I let my hands trail up my legs and over my hips as I straighten.

He speaks so quietly, so gruffly, I almost don't hear him when he says, "Don't move."

He walks toward me, stopping at my feet and looking over my entire back side. His gaze is scorching. Or is it just my mind?

He leans in and I think he's going to touch me, but he doesn't. He stretches across the bar and grabs a bottle of Jack from the shelf beneath it.

I'm watching him from above, every nerve in my body alive and waiting for him to touch me. But still he doesn't. Instead, his eyes locked on mine, he unscrews the bottle of Jack and pours a shot.

"Turn around," he commands.

Tingling with excitement, I do as he asks, stopping myself from crossing my arms over my chest self-consciously. I stand proudly before him, too eager for what's ahead to feel overly insecure.

"On your knees."

I sink to my knees on the bar in front of him. His dark eyes embody everything naughty and sexy and dirty and hot and taboo that I can think of, and I feel the warmth of them all the way to my core. I'm so ready for him, I ache from the neck down.

"Spread your legs."

Edging my knees apart, again I do as he asks. I watch his eyes as they skim over my breasts, down my stomach, and stop right between my legs. I swear I can actually feel him there, feel his tongue, feel his fingers, feel him moving inside me. I gasp, thinking I can't take it one more second, but then his gaze flickers back up to mine.

He hands me the shot glass. "Don't swallow it."

I take the liquid into my mouth and hold it there, watching him, waiting for him to speak, wondering what comes next.

"Now open your mouth. Slowly. Let it run out. Down your chin."

I part my lips and let the fiery liquid ooze from between them. It trickles down my chin and throat, veering to the left and traveling over my nipple then dripping off onto my left thigh. From there, the stream starts to drift inward, toward my center. Cash bends forward and stops it with his tongue.

Starting just to the side of my knee, he licks the liquor from the inside of my leg all the way up to the bend at my thigh. He traces the crease there, coming dangerously close to the throbbing that never seems to cease when he's around. But he stops just shy of it, just shy enough to make me feel like screaming. He laps his way up my stomach to my nipple, where he licks and sucks until every drop of alcohol is in his mouth.

Still not laying a hand on me, Cash reaches to my side and pours another shot. He hands it to me. "Again."

I repeat the steps, only this time Jack dribbles from my chin straight down the center of my chest, between my breasts and over my stomach.

The first drop that slides through the short hair between my legs hits my hot, sensitive flesh like a tingle of electricity. I let the rest of the liquid flow past my lips, hyperaware of the stream that's pouring between my legs.

Reaching out with his hand, Cash moves one finger between my legs, wetting it in the whiskey that's collecting there. His eyes rise to mine as he slips that finger into his mouth.

"Mmm, that's good," he purrs. He bends his head and kisses the inside of my thigh. "But not nearly as good as you." With one long stroke, he licks the opening between my legs. "I didn't even want to think about never tasting you again," he whispers. His mouth is so close to my wet body, I can feel his warm breath. "Oh, God! The way you taste . . ."

Planting his hands on my inner thighs, Cash pushes them

farther apart and presses his mouth against me. With one quick thrust, his tongue is inside. If I were standing I would collapse. The whiskey was like electricity, but this . . . this is like lightning.

I reach out and thread my fingers into his short hair, holding him to me as he moves his lips and tongue, sucking and licking and penetrating me over and over again.

I'm straining against him, moving my hips against his face. The familiar aching tension is building within me when he suddenly stops.

I could cry. Or scream.

"Not yet, baby," he says softly, putting his hand in the center of my chest and pushing. I turn and lie back on the bar. Cash hops up onto it, settling between my legs. "I want you coming on me, while I'm filling you up, stretching you tight."

He bends each of my knees until my feet are flat on the bar and then I feel his tongue again, probing me, making hot circles over the most sensitive parts, giving me stabbing thrusts in the others. He works first one, then two fingers into me, crooking them and rubbing me from the inside as he pulls them in and out of me.

Within seconds, I'm right back where I was—riding the cusp of an impending orgasm.

Again, he stops. Just before I tip over the edge. My breathing is ragged and so is his as he moves forward, scooting his knees under my hips and grabbing my arms to pull me up onto him, my legs on the outside of his.

Like two pieces of a perfectly engineered puzzle, I fit perfectly against him, his hard length sliding between my folds, caressing me, teasing my opening. He crushes my hips to his, reaching down between us to move his still-wet fingers over me.

"What would you say if I told you they could see us?" he says, tipping his head to the side, toward the bank of glass to my left. My heart hammers in my chest. "What if I told you the mirror is only effective when the lights are on up here? What if I told you they could see us if they bothered to look up? Would that turn you on?" He pushes his fingers inside me and I feel my body squeeze them, pulling at them, craving the penetration. "Oooo, you like that, don't you? You like the thought of maybe getting caught, of maybe being seen, don't you?"

With his hands on my hips, he holds me still, his head poised right at my entrance. "Tell me you like it," he instructs.

Breathing heavily, nearly ready to beg him, I admit the excitement that he already knows I feel. "I like it."

Sharply, he pulls me down and flexes his hips, thrusting into me. I can't stop the cry of pure pleasure that bursts from my lips. "How would you feel about them seeing your beautiful body? Them seeing me licking you and touching you?" As if to make his point, Cash pulls my nipple into his mouth and sucks. Hard.

I slide my fingers through his hair and clench them, tugging him closer to me as he urges my body into a rhythm.

"Do you like the thought of someone watching you ride me? Watching you slide up and down on me? Watching your face when you come for me? Watching your mouth move as you say my name, over and over again?"

His words! Damn him and his words! They make me forget that I care about anything. I can't think. I can only feel—feel his fingers biting into my hips, feel his mouth at my chin, his lips at my throat, his teeth at my nipple, feel his breath, feel his body driving into mine.

"You like that, don't you, baby? You like for me to talk to you, to make you tell me things?"

"Yes," I answer breathlessly.

He braces my hands on his chest as he leans back, flexing his hips beneath me as I ride him, allowing my body to slide down even farther over his.

"Oh, damn! So deep," he moans.

I rise up and fall down on him, feeling each penetration pounding through me. Cash leans back on one elbow and brings his other hand between us to touch me. With his thumb, he rubs me. The air leaves the room and I can't breathe. I'm panting, saying things, all sorts of things. I don't even know what kinds of things, but I know they're dirty things and I know Cash loves it.

"I know that feels good. I can feel you sucking at me, getting tighter. So. Tight," he breathes. "Tell me you like it."

"Oh God, I love it."

"Tell me what you want. I want to hear you say it."

"I want," I begin, unable even to finish the thought.

"Say it, baby. Tell me."

"I don't want you to stop. I want you to make me come."

Cash groans and moves his fingers faster, in small tight circles, each stroke ratcheting my body up higher and higher.

"You want me to make you come? I'll make you come so hard, you can't say anything but my name," he forces out through gritted teeth.

Cash sits up suddenly, rolling forward and sliding me beneath him. He grabs one of my legs behind the knee and pushes it up against my chest. Forcefully, he pushes into me. Once, twice, and then I'm exploding.

Spasms rack my entire body, bringing with them a cascade of sensation—wave after wave of it—that I've never before experienced. I can't open my eyes. I can't find my breath. I can't move. I can only feel as I hear myself saying Cash's name. Over and over and over again.

THIRTY

Cash

Olivia is sprawled out on top of me. I rolled us over shortly after we caught our breath so I wouldn't crush her. I'm sure, to her, I feel like I weigh a ton. Not so at all with her. If it weren't for her warmth, I'd almost forget she was there. She's light as a feather.

As she has a habit of doing, she's tracing my tattoo. She sighs.

"You ever gonna tell me what all this is about?" She sounds contented, satisfied. I can hear it in her voice. She might as well be purring.

"If you look closely enough, you can see all the separate elements of the story." I take my finger and trace each part as I explain to her what it all means. "These are the flames that burned up that boat. And my life. These are the wings that flew away with the family I once knew. This is sort of my version of the yin and yang symbol, for me and my lost twin. And this rose is for my mother. May she always rest in peace."

"What's this?" she asks, running her finger over the lettering that winds around my bicep, just below where the flames start. It's unintelligible now. The bullet grazed part of it.

"It used to say *never forgotten*."

"And this wound messed it all up."

I put one arm behind my head and look down at her. She drags her liquid eyes up to mine. "It's fine. And it was worth it."

She closes her eyes, like she's shutting out something painful. "You could've been killed," she says quietly.

"Hey," I say, waiting until she opens her eyes to look at me. "Now you know that I mean it when I say I'd take a bullet for you. Olivia, I love you. I'd gladly take a bullet or a knife or an ass-kicking or . . . whatever to keep you safe." Her emerald eyes glisten with unshed tears. "That's not supposed to make you sad or upset."

"It doesn't," she says on a trembling voice. "It just makes me happy, hearing you say those words."

"It does?" I grin.

She grins in return. "Yeah. Maybe a little."

I run my fingers up her side to tickle her, and I find that she's sticky. "As much as I'd love to stay here with you for a few more days, I suppose we'd better get downstairs and let you clean up. You're a sticky mess."

"I wonder why?"

"I'm not exactly sure, but if you really need to know, we

could try to recreate several scenarios until we discover the one that caused you to get so . . . sticky."

"Promise?"

"Hell yeah, I promise!"

I peck her on the lips and smack her on the ass before I help peel her chest off mine. I do my best to ignore the way her nipples tighten with the stimulation. I feel that telltale twitch between my legs that says some parts of me *can't* ignore it. Her next comment, however, effectively crushes any sign of a boner.

"So what's the deal with Nash and Marissa?"

"Don't know. Don't care."

"Really? You don't care about what happens with Nash?"

I shrug. "It's not like I wish the guy dead or anything, but he's not much like the brother I remember."

"Maybe you two just need some time to get reacquainted with each other, with the men you've become."

I shrug again. "Maybe."

But I'm not making any promises!

We get dressed, head back downstairs, and make our way back to my apartment. When I open the office door, I'm a little surprised to see Marissa sitting on the sofa.

"What are you doing here?"

"Waiting on . . . Nash." She stumbles over his name, which lets me know without asking that she realizes what's going on. Well, at least that part of it, not all the other details.

"He's not back yet? He was supposed to be right behind me."

"I haven't seen him. Neither has Gavin."

Prickles of suspicion raise the hairs at the back of my neck.

"I'll call him and find out where he's at," I tell Marissa, pulling out my cell phone. *And find out what the hell's going on.*

I select his number from the recently dialed list and I wait for it to ring on the other end. When it does, I hear a muffled ring coming from the next room. I think for a second it must be one of the burner cells Olivia and I have been using.

Probably that damn Ginger.

But then I hear the ring of the line against my ear again followed directly by another muffled ring in the next room. Taking the phone with me, I walk back into my apartment. I hear the ring again and it sounds like it's coming from the bedroom. I head that direction.

When I round the corner, I hear the ring tone again. It sounds much clearer. The interior of my bedroom is pitch black since there are no windows to let in even street light or moonlight. I flick the switch to cut on the overhead light and there, lying unconscious on my bed, is a bloody Nash.

I hear someone gasp behind me. If I had to guess, I'd say it was Marissa. She seems to be in some sort of altered state, probably shock related.

But wouldn't it be a freakin' miracle if this whole ordeal unbitchified her?

I turn to see her peeking around me, her hands covering her mouth, her eyes wide and terrified.

"Ohmigod! What have they done to him?"

Much to my surprise, she squeezes past me and rushes to his side. She stands there looking down at him, her head going back and forth as she appraises him from head to toe and back again. But she doesn't move otherwise. I'm sure, with her upbringing, Marissa has no clue what to do at this very moment. I'm just impressed that she'd even *try* to be concerned.

I walk to the head of the bed and look my brother over. His face is busted up pretty bad. He'll look like a damn rainbow in the morning. A puffy rainbow, that is.

His knuckles are in bad shape, too. I can't help but smile that he probably gave *somebody* one hell of a fight. It's when I get to his abdomen that I get concerned. His black leather jacket has fallen away from his side and I can see the wetness staining his black T-shirt. I can also see the jagged slash in the material, revealing bloody skin and a slit in his side beneath it.

"Olivia, take Marissa and go get Gavin. He's working the bar in your place."

From the corner of my eye, I see Olivia spring into action. Marissa, however, is still standing beside me, looking like a deer caught in someone's headlights.

"Marissa!" I shout sternly. She jumps like I startled her. She turns her confused eyes on me. "Go with Olivia."

She nods almost robotically and turns to let Olivia lead her from the room. I notice that as she walks away, she keeps looking back at the bed.

This will push her over the edge for sure. If she's not already batshit crazy, this ought to take care of it.

I turn my attention back to Nash. I check his pulse, which is strong. I feel a rush of relief. I didn't want to alarm the females, but when I first looked at him, I wondered if he was dead. I might not have much fondness for this new Nash, but it would still hurt like a bitch to lose him a second time.

As easily as I can, I mash on the bones around his eyes and jaw. Nothing feels broken. It's a good thing Davenports have strong bones.

I feel around in his hair to see if I can feel any major head wound, thinking that might be why he's unconscious. I feel a goose-egg-sized bump on the back of his head. From what I know of head wounds, though, swelling out is always better than swelling in.

I make my way down to his side. I peel up his shirt from his stomach and examine what looks like a stab wound. Thankfully it's just oozing bright red blood now, which means it probably didn't nick anything major, like an artery or an organ.

I push gently on his stomach. It still feels soft and I know that's a good sign, too. When my fingers get close to his side, he moans and rolls his head.

"You all right, man?" I ask.

I hear the others come back right before Gavin appears at my side.

"Crikey! Someone beat the shit out of 'im!"

Nash cracks open an eyelid and glares at Gavin. It's funny that he can convey so much feeling in that one small gesture. "Kiss my ass," he mumbles through his swollen, busted lips.

"What the hell happened?" I ask him.

"Somebody caught up with me on the bike. I think it's safe to say you're gonna need a new one."

Shit, shit, shit!

"Do you know who it was?"

"Nah. They came up behind me out of nowhere. Wrecked me then beat the fu—" Nash stops himself, cracking his eyelid again and looking at Marissa and Olivia. "Sorry. Beat the crap out of me while I was on the ground. One of those Russian bastards stabbed me and then they went through my pockets, patting me down."

"What were they looking for?"

"My phone, I think. I keep it in my boot so I won't lose it, though."

I hiss through my teeth.

"What is it?" Olivia asks.

"I thought we'd be safe now. Or at least saf*er*."

"You will be. For a while, anyway. This was just a warning. We've got three days to get them the rest of the copies of the video and they said they'll call it even. If not, they're coming after us."

"But we could go to the cops with it. It could incriminate them!"

"I guess that's not enough to scare them."

Part of me had wondered if it would be enough to be effective in keeping them away. Evidently not.

"Three days, huh?"

"Three days."

"Um, I know whatever you people are involved in is pretty serious stuff, but don't you think we need to get him to the hospital?" Marissa interjects.

"No!" Nash cries. "No hospitals. They keep records. And they call authorities."

"Well, we can't just let you lie here and die."

"No worries, mate. I know a guy," Gavin offers.

"A guy?" Nash asks. "I don't need to be offed. I just need to be patched up."

"Yeah, this guy can do that, too."

I say nothing over the *too* part. I'd say most of Gavin's associates are . . . shady.

"I don't know if he'll come to a place this . . . public, though."

I think for a second. "Think you can travel?" I ask Nash.

He tries to hide his cringe. "Yeah. I'm okay."

"You can go to the condo. We can have him meet you there."

"Why don't we go to my place? That way, I can keep an eye on him afterward," Marissa suggests.

"It's too dangerous," Olivia says.

"Agreed," Nash adds.

"I'll stay, too," Gavin offers. "He's not able to defend himself very well in this state. I can stay for a day or two, watch out for them."

"No need for that. If whoever these people are have already given him an ultimatum, wouldn't it be highly unlikely that they'll attack him again? If they'd wanted to kill him, they could've done so already." Marissa, somehow, is the calm voice of reason. "We'll be all right there by ourselves."

"I thought you'd be staying with your father," Olivia says.

"No. I can't stand to be there. Not with him. I feel like I don't really know anybody anymore."

"Then I'll come and stay with you," Olivia says.

"Absolutely not," I blurt.

"Why not? She can't be alone there with her only protection being someone who's been stabbed."

"You need to stay here with me."

"No, I don't. I'll be fine. They've given us three days. I'm sure they'll leave us alone until then."

"Olivia, I'm not willing to take the risk. End of story."

"End of story, huh? So I have no say in the matter?"

I can see the sparks flying from her eyes. It's a tense situation and her hackles are up. It's kind of a turn-on, but now is neither the time nor the place to be thinking stuff like that.

I force myself to take a deep breath before I respond. "I'm not trying to act like an insensitive dictator, but it's not a good idea for you to go back there right now."

"But it's all right for Marissa?"

"More so than you, yes."

"More so, but not completely?"

"Completely? Probably not."

"Then it's settled. I'm going, too." Olivia turns to Gavin. "Can I ride with you?"

I love Olivia, but at this very moment, I'd like to strangle her. "No, you can't. He'll be staying here and closing up while *we* take Nash to Marissa's."

Olivia looks at Gavin again and he shrugs, giving her the smile that says he's staying out of it.

"Can you have your guy meet us there?"

"I think so. He owes me."

"All right, then." I turn to Nash. "You need help getting to the car?"

"Nah, I got it." He says it casually, but I can see the sweat popping out on his forehead as he tries to push himself upright. When he manages to haul himself to his feet, Olivia gets on one side and Marissa on the other and they help him navigate the short distance from the bedroom to the car where it's parked in the garage. As he's hobbling past me, I see his lips twitch.

That bastard's enjoying this!

While that might be funny if it were someone else, with him, I'm not laughing. I don't want him touching Olivia. I don't want him near her, actually. It's irrational and probably more than a little related to jealousy, but I don't care. It is what it is. Doesn't change the way I feel about it.

I grit my teeth until they have him situated in the backseat. All he lacks is a kiss on the forehead from both of them.

I feel like cussing.

Marissa parked in the side alley, so I wait for her to pull out and I follow. No one in the car says a word all the way to the apartment. When we're parked, both girls scramble to fawn all over Nash again, which makes me feel like rolling my eyes. But I don't. I'm not that stupid. If caught, it would only make me look like a jerk, which, at this point, I am. At least toward Nash. I know he's enjoying this. He's probably enjoying setting my teeth on edge as he leans on Olivia.

Prick.

"Keys," I say to Marissa as I pass her. She hands them over and I walk ahead to unlock the door. I push it open and pause for a second to listen. When I hear nothing, I flip on the light switch to the right and look around. It looks exactly like it did a few nights ago when I came back to get Olivia's stuff. That's a good thing.

I guess I could kick shit out of the way, make it an easier path for Nash to navigate. But then I think of that smug twist of his lips and decide it might serve him right if he falls on his arrogant ass.

I look back to the door. The three of them are just standing there. "Well?" I prompt.

I see Nash and Olivia take a step forward. Marissa does not. Olivia looks over at her. "You know you don't have to do this. You can go back to your dad's. Or back to Cash's. No one would blame you if you never wanted to come back here again."

I gotta hand it to Olivia. She nailed it. Marissa looks scared shitless. She's normally pale, but she looks almost dead in the low light.

Her eyes dart around the entryway and back to Olivia. I hear her take a shaky breath. I'll admit, if this is an act, Marissa's good. Damn good. Better than I would've given her credit for.

"No, I need to do this. I can't live afraid forever. Get back on the horse, right?" she says with a weak smile.

"I'll take Nash. You take your time."

Marissa takes a deep breath and shakes her head. "No, I'm okay."

Maybe it's a family thing, that ability to physically convey the idea of picking oneself up by the bootstraps, because Marissa's doing what I've seen Olivia do a few times. She's picking herself up by her bootstraps. Maybe she's got enough of Olivia in her to make her a half-decent human being after all.

The three make their way into the apartment. By the time they reach the living room, I think Nash is supporting Marissa more than she's supporting him.

"This way," she says, steering them toward her bedroom. "He can have my room. I'll take the couch."

No one argues, least of all me. This wasn't my idea. I'm sure as hell not taking the couch. My place is with Olivia. Marissa's on her own.

When the girls start taking Nash's coat and shirt off, I make an excuse to go wait for Gavin's man. It sounds stupid, but it infuriates me to see her taking another man's shirt off, even if that other man is my twin brother. In fact, that might make it worse. It's like she's doing it to me. Only not.

I'm pacing in front of the open front door, feeling testy as hell by the time a nondescript dark sedan pulls up at the curb. A short man gets out, casually looks around, slings some sort of bag over his shoulder, and walks slowly up the sidewalk. When he reaches me, I'm surprised by his youth.

"Where's the hurt one?" he asks flatly. Young or not, this guy is all business.

"And you are?" He might think I'm stupid, but he'd be mistaken.

"Delaney. Gavin asked me to come."

"You a fly buddy of his?"

"No. Worked with him in Honduras."

I've heard Gavin mention that place a couple of times. Apparently he was one of a few . . . specialists hired for some sort of job there. It went all to hell. Just from what little I've heard him say, for mercs it was like being in the trenches during wartime. If this guy was with him, I can see how they could've become indebted to one another.

"This way," I say, taking him back to Marissa's room.

We all stand around like curious onlookers as he patches Nash up. He must have a pharmacy and one hellacious emergency kit of some kind in that bag of his. He gives Nash a couple of shots and cleans his wound with some sort of solution he has to pop open in a tube to use. He sticks a needle full of something else (my guess would be lidocaine or something like that) into Nash's stab wound, then breaks out some sterile gloves and sutures to stitch him up.

When he's done, he sets a bottle of pills on the nightstand, tells Nash to take one three times a day for two weeks, then nods to him and gets up to leave.

I walk him to the door, mainly because I still don't trust the guy. He steps onto the stoop, turns back to give me one curt nod, and then just walks away. That's it.

Killers—they're a different breed. That's for sure.

I wait until the females are done fussing over Nash before I make any suggestions.

"Well, I guess it's time we all get some rest."

"Marissa, are you sure you won't take my bed? You've been through so much . . ."

She smiles at Olivia, obviously touched by her offer. "No, I think I'll stay with him a little longer. You two go ahead."

"Are you sure?"

"I'm positive. That couch is really comfortable, anyway."

"It really is," Olivia agrees. They smile at each other, sharing some sort of inside joke, it seems. It makes me respect Olivia that much more that she can so easily and readily bury the hatchet with someone who's treated her so badly. But that's just who she is. It's part of what makes her so incredible.

"All right, I guess we'll head to bed, then. I need a shower and then I'll probably be out like a light."

"Good night," Marissa says, walking around the bed to perch on the side opposite Nash. "Hey, Liv?"

Damn! We were almost home free, I think as Olivia stops near the door.

She turns to look at Marissa. Again, it seems even I can see the difference in Marissa. Maybe this was just the thing she needed to jerk a knot out of her ass.

"Thanks."

They share another look. Olivia smiles. Marissa smiles. "That's what family's for."

Finally, we escape Nash and Marissa. Olivia doesn't say much, just gathers up some stuff and takes it into the bathroom. A few minutes later, I hear the shower cut on. A few minutes after that, I hear it shut off. Being the guy that I am, I'm a little pissed that I wasn't invited. Of course, I could've just gone in and joined her, anyway, but if she's still irritated with me, that wouldn't be the wisest move.

I take off my clothes, climb into bed, and turn out the lights, settling in to await her. We're going to hash this out before morning, one way or the other.

Quietly, the bathroom door opens. Her room is very dark and the door is closed, so I can't see her, but I can hear her light footsteps as she approaches the bed. Gently, she peels back the covers and eases in beside me. I wait until she gets comfortable before I speak.

"There's something I want you to understand," I begin. I hear her sharp inhalation. "What?"

"You scared the crap out of me!" Olivia exclaims.

"Did you think I'd just go right to sleep, knowing you're upset?" When she doesn't answer, I can only assume it's because she *did* think that. And that pisses me off.

"I just don't understand how you could care so little about what happens to Marissa," she finally says.

"There are several reasons, actually. One, I know what she's like. Two, I can't so easily forget the way she's treated you. And three, she's not you. I'm sorry, but you're my first priority."

"Even so, how could you have let her come here alone, knowing it's not entirely safe?"

"Olivia, she's a grown woman. She can do whatever she wants to. And it's not like she had nowhere safe to go. She could've stayed with her father. She just didn't want to."

"I just don't see how you could be so cold about it."

"I can tell you how. This isn't about Marissa. It never was. It's about you. Keeping you safe. I'm not in love with her. I'm in love with you. Can't you understand that I don't want to live without you? That I *can't* live without you? What the hell would I do if something happened to you? I couldn't let you come here with her by yourself. I couldn't take the risk. I'll *never* take the risk if the risk is losing you. Never. Why can't you understand that?"

I've gotten louder in my agitation, which makes the silence when I'm done much more pronounced.

She doesn't respond, but I feel the bed shift as she moves. Then I feel her hands on my stomach, soft and warm. "Cash?" she whispers.

"Yeah?"

Her hands slide up my chest and circle my neck as she stretches out on top of me. She presses her lips to mine in a featherlight kiss. "That's all you had to say."

"You didn't give me a chance to say it," I mumble against her mouth.

"Next time, lead with that," she says. I feel her lips spread against mine. I know she's grinning.

Quickly, I coil my arms around her and roll her onto her back, settling between her spread legs. She's naked and it takes all of my self-control not to plunge right into her. Her body beckons me like a warm bath on a cold night. Her soul beckons me like a refreshing oasis in the dry desert. And her heart beckons me like a safe harbor beckons a lost ship.

"You mean lead with the fact that I'm in love with you?" I

say as I tease her entrance with my already stiff and throbbing head.

"Yes. Always, always lead with that."

"I'm in love with you, Olivia Townsend," I whisper as I ease into her. I feel her sigh and I echo it.

"I'm in love with you, Cash Davenport."

I pull out of her until only my tip rests within her, and then I slide back in, a little deeper this time. "Promise you'll never leave me. Stay with me, Olivia. Come home with me tomorrow and stay."

She pauses, but only for a second. When she speaks, I can hear the smile in her voice.

"I'll stay with you as long as you want me."

"I'll want you with me forever. I never want to spend another night without you. Ever. I can't stand the thought of something happening to you. I can't stand the thought of us fighting. I can't stand the thought of you being anything other than deliriously happy. With me."

"Then consider me deliriously happy. With you. Always."

"Always," I repeat as I cover her mouth with mine. She sighs again as I move inside her. This time, I breathe it in, her breath becoming a part of me as much as she herself has become a part of me. It's like breathing in life, vitality. Wholeness. And that's how I feel. Finally.

Whole.

Nash

Between waking up in a strange place and the drugs that damn back-alley doctor gave me, I'm a little disoriented when I open my eyes. The first thing I notice is that there's a great-smelling woman curled up against my side. The second thing I notice is that her leg draped over mine has given me a raging hard-on.

Details of what happened and where I am come back in a slow trickle. I'm not in much pain, which surprises me. I figured that bastard probably stuck me with a knife dipped in horse shit or something. But I feel pretty all right as far as that goes.

Until I hear the familiar voice of my brother from the other room, that is. He's talking quietly on the phone.

"Did you do this?"

A pause.

"You know exactly who this is," he growls. "Did. You. Do. This?"

Another pause.

"Trust you? You're crazier than—"

I hear a sigh that turns into another growl before he mutters, "What the hell are we gonna do now? I have to make adjustments to protect the people I love."

It doesn't take a genius to figure out what he's talking about—my little motorcycle accident. Cash worries too much about everyone else.

But not me.

I have one mission. Just one. And it's looking more and more like my plans to destroy the organization that took Mom's life will be a solo effort.

If there's one thing I've learned in life since I left home seven years ago, it's that I can trust no one.

And that includes family.

To be continued . . .

A few times in life, I've found myself in a position of such love and gratitude that saying THANK YOU seems trite, like it's just not enough. That is the position that I find myself in now when it comes to you, my readers. You are the sole reason that my dream of being a writer has come true. I knew that it would be gratifying and wonderful to finally have a job that I loved so much, but I had no idea that it would be outweighed and outshined by the unimaginable pleasure that I get from hearing that you love my work, that it's touched you in some way or that your life seems a little bit better for having read it. So it is from the depths of my soul, from the very bottom of my heart that I say I simply cannot THANK YOU enough. I've added this note to all my stories with the link to a blog post that I really hope you'll take a minute to read. It is a true and sincere expression of my humble appreciation. I love each and every one of you, and you'll never know what your many encouraging posts, comments, and e-mails have meant to me.

http://mleightonbooks.blogspot.com/2011/06/
when-thanks-is-not-enough.html

Keep reading for an excerpt from
the next Bad Boys book

EVERYTHING FOR US

Available in September 2013 from Berkley Books

ONE

Nash

It's always the same. The dream starts out with the feeling of a weight being lifted from my arms. That's how I know what's coming, that I'll look down at my feet and see my hands pulling away from the box of supplies I was carrying, the box that now rests on the faded planks of the dock.

I straighten and take my cell phone from my pocket, flicking my thumb over the button that brings the screen to glowing life. I hit the camera app and raise the phone until I see the girl framed perfectly inside the lighted square.

She's lying on the top deck of a yacht across the way. It's swaying gently against the dock at the marina. It's a great boat, but it's not the boat that I'm interested in. Not at all. I'm interested in the girl. She's young, she's blond, and she's topless.

Her skin is shiny with tanning oil, and the sun glints off

the firm, round globes of her tits. They're the perfect handful, the kind that begs to be squeezed until she moans. The breeze picks up and, although it's warm, her nipples pucker against it. They're pouty and pink and they make my dick throb.

Damn, I love the marina!

Someone bumps my shoulder and I lose the girl in my viewfinder. I turn and glare at the old man who's ambling off down the pier. I bite back the snide comment that's hanging on the tip of my tongue. Cash wouldn't bother. He doesn't hold his tongue for anybody. But I'm not Cash.

Ignoring the old man, I turn back toward the yacht, back toward the topless girl with the great rack. But before I can find her again, something else catches my attention.

There's a man standing at the end of the walkway, at the edge of the shore. He's lounging against the back wall of the little shack that sells basic grocery items and gas for the various watercraft that use the marina. He looks casual enough, but there's something about the way he's dressed that seems . . . off. He's wearing slacks. Like, dress slacks. And he's pulling a thin rectangle out of his pocket. For the most part it looks like a cell phone. Only it's not. With the magnification of my camera, I can see that it's just a plain black box with a little red button on top.

I see his thumb slide easily over the button just before something slams into me so hard it knocks me off my feet and into the water behind me.

Then there's nothing.

I don't know how many minutes, or hours, or even days

have passed when I wake up in the water. I'm floating face up as my head bumps repeatedly against the nubby, barnacle-covered pier.

Achy, I urge my muscles into motion and roll onto my stomach. Stiffly, I ease into a slow swim toward one of the several ladders that dot the length of the dock. I climb, dripping wet, out of the water and look around for whatever caused the loud explosion I heard just before I was thrown into the water.

When I turn toward where my family's schooner was tethered, I see a cluster of people gathered there. It takes a full thirty seconds for my mind to interpret what I'm seeing—an empty boat slip, pieces of flaming wood peppering the dock, bits of splintered furniture scattered throughout the water. And smoke. Lots of smoke. And whispers, too. And, in the distance, growing closer, sirens.

I come awake from the nightmare with a start, just like I always do. I'm sweating and breathing hard, just like I always am. My face is wet with tears, just like it always is. It's been so long since I've had the dream, I forget how devastated and empty and . . . *angry* it leaves me feeling.

But now I remember. I remember with perfect clarity. And today, it's like pouring gasoline onto a raging fire.

I sit up in the bed to catch my breath. My side twinges in pain, reminding me of what happened last night. All of it comes rushing back, further fueling my fury.

Until a small, cool hand touches my shoulder.

I turn to see Marissa sitting up behind me, leaning on her elbow, looking at me through sleepy, sexy blue eyes. Before I can even think about what I'm doing, all the bitterness, all the anger, all the pent-up aggression gets channeled into pure lust. The need to devour something, to lose myself in something overwhelms everything else and I dive in. To her.

Spinning, I roll onto Marissa, pressing her warm body into the mattress. I hear her soft gasp as I crush her lips beneath mine. I swallow it—the sound, the fear, the hesitant desire— taking it in and letting it feed the animal inside me.

My tongue slips easily into her mouth. She tastes sweet, like honey. I push my knee between her thighs and they part, allowing me to settle my hips against hers.

It's not until I push my hand under the edge of her shirt that I realize she's stiff. I lift my head to look down at her. She's staring at me with wide, surprised, slightly terrified eyes.

ABOUT THE AUTHOR

New York Times and *USA Today* bestselling author **M. Leighton** is a native of Ohio. She relocated to the warmer climates of the South, where she can be near the water all summer and miss the snow all winter. Possessed of an overactive imagination from early in her childhood, Michelle finally found an acceptable outlet for her fantastical visions: literary fiction. Having written more than a dozen novels, Michelle enjoys letting her mind wander to more romantic settings with sexy Southern guys, much like the one she married and the ones you'll find in her latest books. When her thoughts aren't roaming in that direction, she'll be riding wild horses, skiing the slopes of Aspen, or scuba diving with a hot rock star, all without leaving the cozy comfort of her office. Visit her on Facebook, Twitter, and Goodreads and at mleightonbooks .blogspot.com.